When night falls, and colors sleep, we walk the land of shadows

But never alone

JG Adams

SHADOW

SHAMANS

A novel

SHADOW SHAMANS

Copyright 2010

JG Adams

JG Adams book titles may be purchased for business or promotional use, or for special sales. For information, email: editor@authorjgadams.com.

http://www.authorjgadams.com/#!/shadow-shamans

ISBN 0—9844674—3—2

978—0—9844674—3—3

Second printing   October 2012

Visit the author's website at:

www.authorjgadams.com

Acknowledgements

I want to acknowledge those that have given me tremendous help creating this novel.

To my first editor, Don McPeak - this work would never have seen the light of day without your guidance and insight.

To my first reader, Danny Giles - your encouraging words kept me going through countless rewrites.

To my proofreaders, Lacretia Garrett, Casey Norton, and Ken Nichols - your comments and sharp eyes helped make this work something I am proud to present.

To my son, JD, whose misplaced, never-ending, confidence in my ability pushed me to become better than I was.

And to Sheila, who gave me the permission and encouragement to look into those hidden places that eventually came to light in the pages of this book.

This book is dedicated to my shaman:

Sheila

CHAPTER 1

3:27 pm

God, I don't want to die!

Ty's chest tightened, and he loosened his tie.

God, I wish I were not here right now. I wish I were on the ground looking up.

Ty hated pain, but detested fear even more. The fear of pain caused him to break into a sweat.

He remembered as a child it took a doctor, two nurses, and his mother to extricate him from under an examination table. He shuddered at the memory of the needle dimpling his skin before penetrating, then sliding through flesh until it struck bone.

At least it's not night!

Fear in the loneliness of night was unbearable…and then there was the granddaddy of all fears — the fear of dying.

When did I get to be so old?

He wiped the sweat from his hands.

I never thought it would end like this. Please, no pain. If I could kiss Lily one more time…give my kids one more hug.

Oh God, I don't want to die!

If I had known it would end today, I would have sipped my coffee instead of gulping it. I would have watched that hawk soar longer.

Oh God, no pain. Please, no pain!

All the hours in church...all the prayers...all the Sunday school classes. I thought I was prepared for this.

Ahead of Ty lay everything he dreaded. The terrible unknown, where faith is proven valid reality or cruel hoax. He looked out to see azure blue sky.

I wonder if I will be able to see sky tomorrow. I wonder if I will be able to see anything.

CHAPTER 2

"It's gone!" Blades said.

"What's gone?"

"The whole damned thing!"

"What thing?" Ty said, his vocal cords stretched to their limit.

"The engine."

"What do you mean?"

Ty felt the vice on his chest tighten.

"Fuel's pouring out," Blades continued.

"Which engine? Shut down the fuel pump!"

"I did. Fuel's still pouring out. Number two."

Ty pressed the radio transmit button. "Mayday! Mayday! Mayday! Atlanta Center, six three Quebec heavy, mayday!"

"They don't work."

"What doesn't work?"

"The radios. They don't work."

"Why not?"

Ty moved the switch to the standby radio. "Mayday! Mayday! Mayday! Atlanta Center, six three Quebec heavy, mayday!"

"Look," Blades said. "The transponder light isn't blinking."

Ty looked at the transponder light. When air traffic control radar swept the airplane, the transponder would normally flash. The small red light did not blink. He moved the switch to activate the standby transponder, but the light on it remained dark.

"The lightening strike and explosion - it knocked out our radios," Blades said as he hit the instrument panel with the heel of his hand.

The left engine surged once, and then shut down.

"What was that?"

"We lost fuel to number one."

The altimeter passed through 28,000 feet as the airplane descended toward the Smoky Mountains.

Ty pulled back on the yoke to slow the airplane and reduce the rate of decent. At 200 miles per hour, the airplane shuddered, rolled right, and entered into a spin. He pushed the yoke away while turning it to the right, and pressed the left rudder pedal. The airplane started flying again, and Ty turned the plane back toward the west.

The altimeter passed through 18,000 feet.

"Let's not do that again," Blades said. "That cost us 10,000 feet, but we're OK."

Ty loosened his grip on the control yoke. "Let's put down some flaps."

Blades moved the flap handle and the airplane rolled to the right again.

"Split flaps! Split flaps!" Ty yelled.

Blades pulled the flap handle up and the plane

stopped rolling, then returned to wings level flight.

Ty wiped the sweat from his forehead.

The altimeter passed through 16,000 feet.

Blades looked out the copilot's side window at the right wing. "That wing is in bad shape. We are in deep trouble."

Ty wiped sweat from his hands on his shirt. The cockpit seemed to close in, and the metal become thinner.

Blades reached for the copilot's yoke. "Let me have it. I can get us through this."

"It's my airplane! I'm in the left seat—"

"Just who do you think you're talking to?" Blades snapped back. "I've got us through tougher times—."

"I swear I'll break your arm," Ty said through clenched teeth. "I'll get it down."

Blades nostrils flared.

"Any kid can do that! I'm talking about walking away from it after—"

"What's that supposed to mean?"

"It means I don't crap my pants when—"

"Back off, Blades!"

The vein that passed across Blades left temple stuck out and his face turned red. "Ever seen me scared? No! Never have! Never will!"

"Back off!"

"You better start thinking about flying instead of dying. I'm better at flying and you're—"

"Shut up, Blades! I'm in charge!"

Blades face turned a deeper red. "Just because you're in the left seat doesn't make you in charge. You—"

"Shut up! It's my airplane!"

The veins on both of Blades temples stood out and his face turned white.

The altimeter passed through 14,000 feet.

"We're going down fast, hot shot," Blades said as he removed his hands from the copilot yoke and leaned back in the seat. "You better pick a spot, quick!"

The green Tennessee Valley lay in the distance. The two hundred mile long valley ran southwest to northeast, the Smoky Mountains forming the eastern border, the Cumberland Plateau the western.

Ty pointed to a green patch in the distance.

"If we can make it over that last ridge…"

"No problem," Blades said as he pushed his back against the seat. "Man, am I glad we don't have any cabin crew pushing the intercom button every ten seconds."

Ty smiled and relaxed for a second. "Yeah, this was supposed to be an easy ferry flight."

"Yep. Don't think we will get any brownie points today."

The altimeter passed through 10,000 feet.

The green ahead disappeared as the airplane approached the mountain ridge.

The altimeter passed through 8,000 feet.

"I don't think we are going to make it."

The altimeter passed through 6,000 feet.

Ty turned the airplane toward a dip in the ridge just before the plane entered a cloud. When they emerged, the airplane was below the top of the ridge.

"We're not going to make it!"

Five seconds before crashing into the mountain, the plane entered an updraft and shot up. Fifteen feet above the ridge the updraft stopped, and the airplane started down. The wings brushed the tops of two trees, and the plane passed into the valley.

Blades let out a long breath. "That was too close."

Ty could see the hills on the other side of the Tennessee Valley, and the French Broad River ahead.

The altimeter passed through 4,000 feet.

"There's a good spot over there," Blades said as he pointed to the right.

Ty turned the airplane to the right and saw a clearing.

"Think we can make it?"

"It's going to be close."

Ty used his right shirtsleeve to blot sweat from his forehead, then from the tip of his nose. His tongue felt like a thick, sticky cucumber crammed inside his mouth.

Blades threw the landing checklist over his left shoulder.

"Won't be needing that."

The checklist hit the door, and then fell onto the floor.

"Hey!" Ty said with a critical look.

Blades grinned. "What? Worried about scratching the airplane?"

Ty frowned.

"So you really think we're going to make it through this?" Blades continued. "We have about as good a chance as a prairie dog in a cathouse."

Ty broke into a grin and then laughed. "A prairie dog in a whore house? Where did you come up with that?"

"I said cathouse. Hells bells, we've come through tougher times than this and—"

"You said we were in deep trouble!"

"We've been in deep trouble before."

"Not this bad."

Blades grin broadened. "Remember when that guy shoved my head into the ceiling fan? You thought I was a goner. This is a walk in the park."

The altimeter passed through 2,500 feet, but the radar altimeter displayed 1,480 feet above the ground.

The windshield felt as if it was inches from Ty's face as he looked out at the ground speeding towards him.

"I don't think this is going to be good," he said as he put his hand back on the yoke.

"Ya' just never know" Blades replied. "But I do believe she's in for a heck of a day."

"I'm not worried about her, I just hope God—"

"God! You had better focus on flying. It's good flying that's got us through, not God. And it was bad flying that got those other fellas killed."

Ty started to push down the flap lever when Blades grabbed his hand. He pulled his hand from the lever.

"Oh, yeah. Habit you know."

Ty looked at the clearing ahead. "How about you call the airspeed?"

"You have two ten now," Blades replied.

Ty could see tree branches rushing underneath them, and he let the airplane sink until it was 50 feet above the ground, then he pulled back on the yoke.

"One ninety."

"One eighty-five."

Uh oh. The meadow isn't so smooth after all. This is not going to be good.

"It's been nice flying with you Ty. I hope that god of yours exists."

Ty felt calm, and the vice on his chest released.

Me, too. Oh god I don't want to die.

The tail touched down, and there was a slight scrape, not the jarring crash he expected. The tail bounced off the tops of the small hills, and as the airplane slowed, the nose dropped. Time stopped as Ty looked at the mountains in the distance.

"This is going to be bad," Blades said as he pulled his legs back against the seat, and grabbed the shoulder harness straps.

The nose of the airplane continued to drop until the plane veered to the left, and the nose lifted up again, and then slammed into the earth.

Ty saw grass—then blue sky—then grass—then—

Silence. Total, complete, devoid, silence. No ringing in his ears, no sound of breath, no cry of fear. Only silence. He had never heard silence before.

So this is death. No big light or choir of angels, no anger, no fright, no joy, no smell, no taste, only silence. And no pain! Wow, no pain.

At 3:42 pm, the journey began.

CHAPTER 3

Day 44

Is this death? Am I alive? Is this a dream? Where am I?

Quiet was replaced by stillness that felt familiar, yet out of place. Ty had sensed this presence before, but could not connect it to any person or place.

Is anyone there? Who are you? Is someone there?

He felt something covering his face, and struggled to focus on what approached.

Who are you?

The veil of fog lifted and he recognized the presence — it was pain!

Oh God, no pain. Please no pain.

Recognition increased the strength of the pain, and it broke through the dike that held it back, flooding through every cell in Ty's body.

This isn't a dream, this is dying!

He succumbed back into the bliss of unconsciousness and welcomed the world of dream that once haunted him.

God, I don't want to go back, I want to stay here. Please don't send me back.

He awoke to buzzing in his ears. The pain had diminished until a rivulet seeped through to consciousness; it's dull ache reviving memories of climbing up on a tubular metal bike rack as a child, and then falling, the cold metal separating and crushing his testicles with his own weight.

Oh God, no more pain. Please no pain.

New pain and smell joined the cacophony of senses that clamored for Ty's consciousness. A hot, acrid smell caused him to gag.

I'm on fire! Oh God, I'm burning!

Panic coiled his chest like a python, but diminished as he drifted back to the refuge of dark void.

Don't make me go back. Please, don't make me go back.

A hint of light penetrated the void and grew until he saw bright specks floating in a sea of red. The acrid smell and burning were gone, replaced by a taste of something sweet. The taste was also familiar, but unrecognizable; he breathed a few shallow breaths and his nose verified what his tongue tasted.

Grass! It's grass! I can smell and taste grass. I'm alive!

He savored the flavor in his mouth.

I didn't expect grass in heaven. What if this isn't heaven?

The light continued to grow and he felt sweat on his face. The sweat trickled down into the corner of his mouth and he sucked it in to wet his parched lips. The sweat tasted heavy and sweet — blood! The combination of pain, and taste of blood, made his stomach churn, but before he could vomit, he lapsed back into darkness.

Why have you done this to me? What have I done? You were supposed to take care of me.

Curses started to form but were lost.

*   *   *   *   *

The void disappeared, and the pain eased, except on his left side. He moved the fingers of his right hand and they brush against a piece of metal. Movement of his right elbow sent flashes of hot pain through his left shoulder.

Where am I? Is anyone there?

Gradually, the memory of the crash emerged and he relived the panic of his last moment. His spirit sank until it hit bedrock, breaking the grip of fear.

Ty tried to bring his hand to his face, but something blocked his arm. When he fingered the

13

object, he felt a piece of metal stuck in dirt. He reached up and felt the back of his head.

This is encouraging.

He felt space above his head, but when he tried to lift his head, something stopped it. Curses formed again.

He put his arm down and scooped away dirt from around the metal piece. After several scoops, a faint light started to filter through. With each scoop, the light became brighter, until his fingers broke through. He wiggled his fingers in front of his eyes.

"Boy, am I glad to see you guys."

The sight of his fingers gave Ty hope and brought a moment of clarity.

All my life I've been afraid. Afraid in good times I would be punished and bad things would happen. Afraid in bad times there would never be good times. Afraid of death. Afraid of life. Afraid of God. Afraid of there not being a God. Afraid of being afraid. But now I'm free to live the life I want to live. I'm no longer afraid — but I need help!

The tunnel underneath the metal was large enough to allow Ty to breathe in fresh air. He listened for voices, but heard only the wind.

"Help! Over here! Help! I'm over here!"

He heard a voice in the distance.

"Over here!" he shouted, but there was no response. "Help! I'm over here!"

Pain shot down his left side as he strained to move his mouth closer to the opening. He heard the voice again.

"Help! I'm over here! Can you hear me? I'm over here."

He turned his head to move his ear closer to the opening and strained to hear a reply.

"Coo, Coo," the dove called.

His hopes tumbled.

"Is there anyone out there? Can anyone hear me? Is there anyone here?"

He rested his head and slipped back into unconsciousness.

CHAPTER 4

Day 43

When Ty awoke it was dark, and he felt a breeze across the back of his neck. Even as a child, he had liked the feel of a breeze on his face. His grandfather told him the wind contained the breath of their ancestors. After the passing of his grandfather, he stood with his face to the wind and wondered how much of his grandfather's breath passed over and around him.

Grandpa, I could use your help now, or is this it? Is this how I will die, my face in the dirt breathing though a tunnel? And if I die, what will eat what's left of me? I hope it's a fox or bear, not a possum or worms.

He felt anger welling inside him, until it erupted in frustration.

"What are you talking about? Quit crying you big baby! Nothing is going to eat you! You have survived forty-five years of flying and you're not going to die now! Life is for living and as long as you have breath, live it!"

Anger fueled Ty's strength, and he reached around to his chest, where he felt the shoulder straps across his chest.

If I can release the harness maybe I could wriggle out.

He maneuvered his arm back around to his

chest and felt for the harness release; each movement causing pain to shoot down his left side. His hand brushed against the release.

Whoa! This could be a bad idea. If I'm hanging by this harness and I open it and drop down...I don't even want to think about the pain that would bring.

He probed around the seat with his right hand until he felt fingers and another hand.

Are those my fingers? Has my hand been cut off? Maybe they're Blades fingers.

He lifted the fingers and pain shot down his left side.

Nope, they're mine. Don't think I want to do that again anytime in the near future.

He continued to explore the small space until he felt the bottom of a fire extinguisher. When he tried to move the extinguisher, a loud explosion rocked the seat, and a thick cloud smothered his face. He gasped for breath as consciousness faded from gray to silence.

*　　*　　*　　*　　*

Ty awoke coughing and gagging. The fire extinguisher dust caused him to choke and sneeze at the same time. After several seconds, the dust cleared and he could breathe again.

Well at least I don't have to worry about the fire extinguisher. I'm getting comfortable talking to myself. Maybe that's not such a good thing.

"Blades! Blades, are you out there?"

No one answered.

"Blades! Can you hear me?"

Ty heard the wind calling as it blew across him. Its gentle fingers pulling, as if trying to free him.

Grandpa, I appreciate you not leaving me alone.

It was dark, but Ty did not feel fear.

I have to get my left arm free if I want to get out of here. Think. Is there any other way? Any way without pain? No, guess not. Well, pain's not the worst thing.

Ty tried to free the fire extinguisher by pushing it from side to side, but there was not enough room to move it very far.

"Wow! That was more work than I thought it would be. I think I'll lie here and rest for just a minute."

CHAPTER 5

It was light when Ty was awakened by a moan.

"Blades! Can you hear me?"

There was no response.

At least he's alive and I'm not alone. Things are getting better. No more rest, I have to get free. If I can just get the seat to move, maybe I can get my arm out.

He rocked the seat to the right and pain shot up his left side, but the seat did not move. When he tried with more force, the seat moved a little, and the pain seemed to lessen.

I think I'll release the harness and take my chances.

He braced himself and released the harness, but nothing happened. He did not move and there was no pain.

That just goes to prove the old Marine Corps adage 'No pain, no gain.'

He then remembered another Marine Corps adage, "Pain is weakness escaping the body."

"I must be one strong fella by now."

Ty felt around the seat with his right hand and found a piece of structural aluminum tubing. When he pulled on the tubing, it broke free.

If I can just get this between the seat and the

fuselage, I might be able to pry the seat away and free my arm.

He passed the tube under his body and forced it into an opening between the frame of the seat and the fuselage. He pulled the tube toward his body with his right arm, and pain shot up his left side. He clinched his teeth and chose to ignore it, as he pulled harder. Nothing moved. He tried a second, third and fourth time, but again nothing moved. When he rocked his body and pulled on the tube, the seat did not move, but he raised the threshold for pain.

There has to be a way out of here, I just haven't discovered it yet. Maybe a longer lever would work. Maybe there's something between my legs.

Ty laughed at the irony of his own words.

"Something useful at a time like this."

He moved his hand and felt a metal object under the seat. When he pulled on it, his body immersed in pain and he rolled to the left.

The seat release! Why didn't I think of that earlier?

He was lying on his back, and through what was left of the pilot's side window, he could see a grassy meadow and sky. His left arm was free and he pulled it away from the seat. Pain radiated with every movement, but subsided when he managed to get his arm in his lap.

"Thank you Jeeesus!" he said with the accent and fervor of a southern preacher.

Blades let out a low groan and Ty turned to the source of the sound.

"Blades, can you hear me? It's me, Ty. I'm over here."

Ty untangled his legs and kicked debris away from his feet. When his feet were free, he used them to scoot his body across the dirt until he could see Blades. What he saw horrified him. A large mass of blood and tissue replaced what was once a face.

The tissue pulsed slightly.

CHAPTER 6

The sight of Blades' face nauseated Ty. He turned away and looked up at the sky.

Don't let him die. I don't want to be alone.

He unbuttoned his shirt, put his left arm inside, and then buttoned the shirt to form a sling. He pushed himself up into a sitting position, the exertion causing him to break into a sweat. He checked his body with his right hand and found that his left arm and right knee hurt, but the rest of his body felt normal.

Using his arm and legs, he scooted closer to Blades, his attention fixated on the pulsating mass of blood and tissue. His thoughts raced about what to do next, when a hole opened in the gelatinous mass.

"Ty. Is that you?"

Blades voice sounded small and muffled.

"Yeah Blades, it's me."

"Ty, I'm thirsty."

Ty looked around for something to drink. "I'll have to find something."

Blades did not respond, but Ty could hear him struggling to breathe. With each breath, a piece of flesh over the hole in Blades' face pushed out, and then sucked back in. He lifted up the piece of flesh and discovered Blades' mouth. Blades breathed easier and He continued lifting the skin until Blades nose, then his eyes emerged. Blades face was clean, and he

25

looked peaceful with his eyes closed. When He lifted the flesh further, he found it covered the wound on Blades head.

Blades, you've been scalped! I've heard stories of people in the old west being scalped, and I think some of them even survived.

He pressed down on Blades hair and the scalp grasped on to bone beneath, causing him to pull back his hand and shudder.

Man, that looks bad, he thought.

He shuddered again.

"I'm thirsty too, Blades. I'll go get us some water."

Blades did not respond.

He shook Blades shoulder with two fingers. "Blades, can you hear me?"

Again, Blades did not answer, but he could hear him breathing. The breaths were deep and long, like a man in restful sleep.

Ty grasped the cockpit wreckage with his right hand and used the metal to pull himself up. His legs were stiff, and his right knee was sore, but the pain was manageable and it felt good to stand. When he turned and saw the rest of the wreckage, he sucked in a quick breath.

The fuselage lay upside down at the end of a long scar in the earth. When the airplane crashed, the nose slammed into the dirt, causing the cockpit to break away and roll across the ground. The open end of the fuselage dug into the earth, and the plane did an end over end flip, and then slid across the meadow, the tail sticking down like a giant boat rudder. The tail carved a deep gouge in the earth, and stopped two feet from what was left of the cockpit. The fuselage had collapsed, and a semblance of the once graceful airplane remained. The wings lay like pieces of a puzzle alongside the gouge in the earth. He felt loss as he looked at what had been beautiful and elegant. The feeling of loss was replaced by thankfulness that no passengers were on board, and that the tail stopped the fuselage from sliding further.

Ty looked down at Blades, who was protected by what was left of the cockpit. He wanted to cover Blades with something for additional protection, and looked for a blanket, or anything else he could use to protect Blades. Thirty feet to his left, he saw what looked like a blanket in a bush. As he walked toward the blanket, the color changed from blue to blue green, and he saw it was a piece of metal.

I can't get a break! Why can't I have a blanket? Where is everybody? Why hasn't anybody come to rescue us? What the hell is going on?

He wanted to hit something but was too tired, and too sore. He started to hobble back to the wreckage when he saw a blanket on the ground a few feet from Blades. The blanket was folded in a square as if it had been placed there.

"How did I miss that?"

As he approached, he saw there was not one blanket, but several. He tried to bend over to pick up the top blanket, but pain in his left side convinced him bending was not an option. His knee prevented kneeling.

"I just can't get a God damned break!"

He looked around for something he could use to pick up the blanket. To his right lay a stick on the ground, and he limped over and stood above the stick.

"Way to go stupid! Just how are you going to pick up the stick? If you could pick up the stick you wouldn't need the stick!"

Ty clinched his hands in anger.

"I'm not going to get angry, and I'm not going to get pissed. I'm going to get even. I'm going to find a way to do this!"

He shook his fist at the sky.

"So there! Take that! I'm not going down so easy! You're not going to beat me!"

He spotted a piece of aluminum tubing sticking up from part of the wreckage. The tubing was wedged between two pieces of metal. He walked over to the tubing, his feet shuffling as if they were hobbled, and he pulled on the tube. It moved, but would not come out. He pulled harder but the tube refused to break free. Ty rattled the tube back and forth in frustration.

"All right, you SOB, you're coming out of there if it's the last thing I do. We can do this the easy way, or the hard way, but you are coming out."

He braced his left foot against the wreckage where it met the ground, and wrapped his right arm around the end of the tube.

"One, Two, Three."

He pulled hard, and the tube broke free, his inertia propelling him backwards where he landed on his left side. An explosion of pain rifled through his body and he opened his mouth, but only a hiss of air managed to sneak past piano wire taut vocal cords. The pain brought back memories of the bicycle rack.

It was minutes before his head was clear, and he saw the bone of his left arm pressing out against the skin.

"Well, now I know where it's broken."

He rolled over onto his back, and the bone in his left arm slid into position. As he sat, the pain in his arm subsided to a dull ache. He picked up his new aluminum cane, took a deep breath, and used the cane to stand.

Ty shook the piece of aluminum at the sky.

"Take that!"

He spread the blanket over Blades.

Walking around the wreckage, he discovered coffee, a coffeepot, peanuts, pretzels, sugar and creamer, but no water or soda. Using the tube, he picked up the coffeepot and looped his belt through the handle.

"I'll be back in a flash, Blades. You just hang in there."

The plain drained to the north, and he could see erosions in the soil.

"Water runs downhill. I just hope it doesn't run downhill a long way."

After a few steps, Ty stopped and looked back at Blades.

"I hope you're still here when I get back, but if you're not, have a good flight. I have your wing all the way."

He turned and walked away with tears in his eyes, not expecting to see Blades alive again.

CHAPTER 7

As Ty walked his knee loosened, but the pain in his left arm worsened. While pushing through a dense thicket of rhododendron, his right shoulder started to ache. After several minutes, he walked into a clearing and saw a log under the shade of a cedar tree. Nature had whittled the logs surface, and it gave a little as he sat down.

Just in time. This feels great! I think I'll stay here for a while.

The midday sun was heating the air, and sweat ran down his face, each trickle a stinging rivulet. His left arm and shoulder throbbed.

"It's going to be a long day."

Ty stretched out on the log, and looked up at the sky through the branches of the tree. He listened to the songs of the birds, and the quiet between their songs. He held his left arm up and the throbbing stopped.

Is this a dream? Where is everybody? Why hasn't anyone come? If this is a dream, it's a bad one.

He drifted off to sleep.

* * * * *

When Ty awoke, he lay on the log until a

muscle in his back started to ache. He sat up and looked at the lush green surrounding him. His knee was stiff, his arm started to throb and the muscle in his back still ached.

This is going to be a very long day, and I'm not so sure tomorrow is going to be any better.

After walking a short distance, he heard the faint sound of running water; the sound became louder with each step. He pushed through a small clump of bushes and emerged on the bank of a stream. Water cascaded over boulders, creating waterfalls and small pools. The air was cool and the clear water inviting.

Ty's mouth salivated. He removed the coffeepot from his belt, waded into the stream, and sat down in the water.

"Oh yeah! This is great!"

Water swirled around him, dissolving pain and carrying it away. He looked down and saw his reflection in the water.

Yikes! What happened to you?

He saw a large gash across his forehead, and his face was covered with dried blood. Through cracks in the dark crust, he could see skin. The left side of his head looked as if it had been shaved, but his ear looked normal. When he touched his face it felt rough, and everywhere he touched hurt.

Ty leaned over and placed his head into the water, and rubbed his face with his right fingertips. After coming up for air several times, he felt smooth skin, and pulled his face from the water.

"Hey, there's the guy I know. There are a few

more wrinkles, and what's left of the hair is whiter, but that's the same guy that's looked back at me for almost sixty years."

Ty placed his face back in the water and drank until he ran out of breath. The water tasted sweet, and felt cool as it flowed down his throat.

He moved to the side of the stream and leaned back against a rock. The stream was lined with rhododendron bushes that provided shade, and he listened to the song of the water as it passed over rocks and into pools. The song reminded him of a poem.

"You must go forward

You must go on,

For the day is ending

And the night is long."

Ty bolted upright. "Oh my God! Blades! I came to get water for Blades!"

He tried to jump up, but his body had stiffened, and it took several tries before he was able to pick up the coffeepot. He filled the pot with water, passed his belt back through the handle, and then tried to scramble up the bank. His right knee refused to bend and he fell backward, the water cushioning his fall.

OK, OK, I'll take it easy.

He used the cane and left leg to work his way up the bank. His right leg remained stiff and straight.

"I can't believe I forgot about Blades. How stupid can I get? I sat there sunning myself while he's waiting for me to come back with water. I can't believe I did that!"

As his clothes dried, his body warmed and his knee began to move easier.

Even though the walk back to the wreckage was uphill, it did not take as long as the outbound journey. Approaching what was once their home in the sky, Ty saw Blades still strapped in his seat.

What if he's dead? What if I'm alone? Please don't let him be dead; I don't want to be alone. Where is everybody? Why has no one come to rescue us?

He removed the coffeepot from his belt and then used the cane to help sit down beside Blades. He held his breath, put his ear close to Blades mouth, and was relieved to hear Blades breathing.

"Blades. Blades, can you hear me? It's me, Ty. Can you hear me?"

Blades did not move.

"I have some water. Do you want a drink?"

He rubbed Blades shoulder. "Come on B, wake up. I have some water."

Blades breathing quickened, the fingers on his left hand moved, and he opened his eyelids, blinking several times as his eyes adjusted to the light.

"Ty, is that you?"

"Yeah, B, it's me."

"What happened? Where'd you go?"

"I went to find water, I'm sorry it took me so long. Are you thirsty?"

Blades licked his lips.

"I'm going to pour some water into your mouth, but you'll have to do the swallowing. OK?"

Bladed nodded.

Ty poured a small amount of water into Blades' mouth, and he tried to swallow, but aspirated water and started to choke.

"OK. That was good for a first time. Are you ready for some more?"

Again, Blades nodded.

As he started to pour, Blades stopped breathing and his throat moved in a swallowing motion. As the water entered his mouth, he swallowed and then started breathing again.

"Outstanding! I think we've got this down to a science."

Blades breathing quickened, his mouth moved and a combination between a moan and a grunt came out.

"I didn't quite get that, try again," Ty said as he put his ear down by Blades mouth.

"Hurts."

Ty pulled back and looked at Blades. "I'll bet it does. Where does it hurt?"

Blades lifted his left arm to his chest. "All over."

He looked at Blades arm and his legs splayed in unnatural positions.

"Does your head hurt?"

Blades shook his head.

The answer surprised Ty.

Wow, your head should be throbbing. If you knew how you look, you might hurt a lot more.

"How about your legs?"

Again, Blades shook his head.

I wonder if he can even feel his legs.

Ty looked at Blades contorted arm. "How about your arms?"

Again, Blades shook his head.

The answered again alarmed Ty.

That arm should be killing him. I wonder if his neck is broken. No, it can't be, he moved his left arm and fingers.

"Does your chest hurt?"

"Yeah."

I can deal with things on the outside, but things on the inside, that's a different story.

Ty's mind raced.

Maybe his back is broken.

"Can you feel your hands and feet?"

Ty was surprised to see Blades move his fingers one by one, then his left foot.

"Yep," Blades whispered.

"And no pain?"

"Nope."

"Blades you are amazing."

Blades lifted his left hand and motioned Ty closer. "Remember the bike rack? Feels worse than that."

Sympathetic pain shot through Ty's groin, and he shuddered, as he remembered what it felt like to have his testicles squashed around a metal tube.

"Man, I'm sorry to hear that. Would you like some more water?"

Blades nodded his head.

Ty fed Blades all the water in the pot, and with each drink, Blades seemed to become stronger.

Ty relaxed and realized his right arm ached from holding the coffeepot. He put the pot down and shook his hand.

"That's it B, the water's gone. I'll go get more, you stay right here."

He started to stand but stopped when he heard Blades whisper something. He rolled back over and put his ear by Blades mouth.

"What did you say?"

"Thank you," Blades whispered as he lifted his left hand and put it on Ty's leg.

The expression of gratitude caused tears to well in Ty's eyes. "You're welcome."

He started back across the meadow to the stream, not noticing the sun low in the sky.

I wonder if Blades will see the light of another day. Please God, don't let him die.

CHAPTER 8

Ty was walking back to the plane when he noticed the sun sinking below the horizon. His pace quickened, but it was dark when he arrived. Blades was still sleeping, and he covered him with another blanket.

Good for you. Healing is what you need right now.

He sat down and watched the last vestiges of sun, his mood sinking with the disappearing light.

God I hate the night! I always hated flying into the sunset. When the sun sets, there is only blackness. And loneliness. I was always going to places far away; far away from everyone I loved, while those below sat down to dinner and then climbed into bed to sleep as spoons or wrestle in passion. For me there was no dinner, no passion, and no caring touch.

"God I hate the night!"

Night belongs to youth with all its passion and danger, all its promise and beckoning. For me it brings loneliness. And death. Death of day, death of colors, death of sight, death of me. God I hate the night!

Cold darkness closed in and Ty knew it was a matter of time before he slipped into the realm of the unconscious. He thought of his wife and children, and longed for their touch, their kisses, and their laughter.

"God I hate all this! I wish it were already day. Maybe they will come for us tomorrow."

He lay down next to Blades, covered himself with several blankets, and then rolled a blanket to form a pillow.

When did I become like this? I used to be a night owl, staying up tinkering, cooking or working until I couldn't keep my eyes open. Maybe even then I didn't want the day to end. Maybe I've never wanted the day to end.

"God I hate the night!"

He did not want this day to end, and feared what tomorrow would bring.

"Why have you done this to me?" he whispered as he laid his head on the pillow. "Why?"

Between waking and sleep, Ty heard a voice whisper.

"What do you want from us?"

What? Who are you?

"What do you want from us?" the voice repeated.

"Who are you? Speak up! I can't hear you."

"What do you want from us?"

Ty was becoming frustrated. "Who are you?"

"We are that voice of night."

"Are you an angel?"

"We are angel. What do you want from us?"

"Are angels real?"

"As you expect, no. But, we are very real. You just never want to see us."

"I've never seen an angel."

"You have seen us many times. We passed you many times a day, yet you did not recognize us. We brushed against your face and laid our hand on your shoulder many times."

"Why are you here?"

"You called us."

"I called you? When did I call you?"

"When you asked why? What do you want from us?"

"I want you to fix it! I want you to make everything back the way it was."

"We don't fix things and the past never returns."

"Then what good are you! What good can you do me?"

"We bring you nothing but blessings. We reassure, comfort and assist as you move through your purpose on earth. What do you want from us?"

"I want to know why."

"All things in good time. This is part of your journey. Do not look back. Do not concern yourself with the future. Look within for the answers you seek."

"Look within? Look within for what?"

The voice did not answer.

"Hello. Are you there? Is anybody there?

Where is everybody?"

CHAPTER 9

Day 42

"Ty! Wake up! Come on, wake up!"

Ty hated voices in his dreams.

"Ty! Wake up!"

"Go away! Leave me alone; you have no right to be here, leave me alone."

The coffeepot hit him squarely on the back of the head.

"Ow!"

"Ty! You have to help me. I'm in pain and need you to cut me loose."

It was almost dawn, but there was enough light that shapes were visible.

"I need to take a leak and I can't get out of this harness."

Ty turned to see the whites of Blades eyes staring at him.

"You're alive!"

"No kidding, and so are my kidneys. Now help me get out of here."

He tried to stand, but the pain in his arm and leg stopped him, so he crawled over to Blades. He tried to release the harness with his right hand.

"It's stuck!"

"Well, cut the straps. There's a knife in my left

pocket."

Ty searched Blades left pants leg and felt a small lump through the fabric. The position of Blades leg made it impossible for him to get his hand in the pocket.

"Can you move your leg? I can't get my hand in your pocket."

"Man I have to go!" Blades said as he straightened his leg. "Hurry up."

Ty tried to force his hand into the pocket without success. "Two good hands would help."

"You're going to have two wet hands if you don't hurry."

"I'm hurrying as fast as I can."

The knife tumbled out on the ground. He opened the blade with his teeth, and with two quick slices, Blades slumped free.

"Ouch!"

Ty cut the remaining straps. "Sorry, you OK?"

"Naw. My right arm is stuck. Man, I have to go. How about helping me out here — never mind. I got it."

Ty heard the sound of Blades unzipping his pants, followed by the sound of water on earth. Steam rose in the cool morning air, and Blades moaned as he urinated.

"Boy, that hurts so good. Sex is good, but nothing beats taking a leak when you really have to go. Damn!"

"You OK?"

"Yeah, I'm OK. Remember not to pee uphill."

Ty smiled. It was the first time he had smiled since before the crash. He rolled onto his back, looked up at the stars, and thought back to when he and Blades were in Vietnam.

"Hey B, remember Vietnam?"

"Vaguely, what about it?"

"Man, you lived life to the fullest. You partied too often, slept too little, and drank way too much."

"Yeah, we had some great times. What do you mean too much?"

"Just about every mission you were drunk or hung over."

"No I wasn't.

"Yeah, right. Then why did you always lead the missions?"

Blades rolled on his back and looked over at Ty. "Because I was the best pilot."

"No, because you were dangerous, and—"

"What do you mean dangerous?"

"You and that helicopter were all over the sky. Everyone else had to stay behind to prevent a midair collision. We couldn't let you follow up the rear, because that's what you might have done. Besides, it was entertaining to watch you try and keep the rotating part up and the wheel side down."

"What are you talking about, I was a good pilot, no, a great pilot."

"Yeah, then why is your name Blades and mine

Ty? Remember how you got the name?"

"Yeah, yeah, I've heard the story a million times."

"When you were plummeting to earth I thought for sure you were dead, but you pulled it out at the last moment, and bounced so high I thought you were going to have to log two landings.

He slapped his thigh and stated to laugh.

"And then when the chopper started meandering around in figure eights…"

Ty grabbed his stomach to keep it from hurting.

"You started…you started chopping down those trees and…"

Laughter broke Ty's speech. "And mowing grass—"

"Yeah, yeah, same old story," Blades replied.

"It hurts," Ty said between fits of laughter. "Oh, God, that was so great."

Ty continued when he regained his composure. "I wanted to name you weed whacker…"

After several minutes, Ty stopped laughing and wiped his eyes. "God that was great."

Ty drifted off to sleep thinking about the war and Blades antics.

CHAPTER 10

Day 41

The sun was a hand above the horizon when its warmth stirred Ty from his sleep. His first movement reacquainted him with injuries, old and new. As long as he did not move, the injuries did not complain. He decided to sit and enjoy the beauty of the morning. The birds were busy and their songs added serenity to the setting. Steam rose from the meadow framed in a border of dark green.

"This is more beautiful than anything captured on canvas or film."

Sunshine reflecting off the coffeepot broke the spell. The shiny work of man lay out of place in this setting. He looked over at Blades, who was sleeping. In the morning light, Blades looked younger. Ty looked down at his own hands and then made a fist to pump fluid out of his swelled fingers.

In spite of everything, I feel good.

He ran his fingertips over the swelling on the back of his head.

Dummy, why didn't you use the coffeepot to urinate in, instead of hitting me with it?

He looked at the meadow again, the trees in the distance obscured by the rising mist.

There's something special about this place, or am I taking time to see the world as it is. I spent so much of my life rushing to meet a deadline or fulfill an obligation. It doesn't make any difference, because

I like it here. It's so peaceful. I'm so peaceful.

His thoughts were interrupted by a growl from his stomach. He used the piece of wreckage he was leaning against to pull himself up; the pain of hunger motivated him more than the pain in his arm. His steps were stiff and mechanical as he searched through the wreckage, finding an unopened box of pretzel packages, and several bags of peanuts. He opened one of the bags of peanuts, emptied the contents into his mouth, and crunched the nuts between his teeth until they melted into a smooth, delicious crème. The pretzels were a good compliment that added balance to the meal.

Nothing like peanuts and pretzels for breakfast. The dream of every seven-year-old American boy.

Several packages of the salty snack stirred a thirst that demanded attention but he did not want to walk to the stream again.

The cool morning air chafed at the cuts on his hands and face. His body protested every move, but the pangs of thirst won over physical ailments. Ty picked up the coffeepot, checked Blades, and then started walking back toward the stream.

The walk to the stream seemed shorter than the day before. He passed a group of robins as they foraged for worms and insects in the grass. A large male raised his head to look at him, while the rest of the group continued to forage without looking up. He felt accepted in their domain, and considered it an honor.

Before reaching the stream, Ty heard the sound of water on its relentless journey back to its birthplace. When he had pushed his way through the last stand of rhododendron, he collapsed next to the water, letting his face immerse in the glistening nectar. The first swallow cooled his parched throat. He continued to drink until he was full, and then lay on the rock next to the water.

He put his hands behind his head and looked up at the sky where he yearned to swim with shiny wings.

God, I wish I were up there looking down on all of this. Not long ago I was in bed with my wife and I should have stayed there. I would have done things differently if I had known. God, I wish I were up there.

Dogwoods hung over the stream and formed a tunnel through which rays of light passed and reflected off the water.

"Wow."

Looking up at the sky brought back memories of being next to a stream with his grandfather as they looked up at the vapor trail of a jet overhead. Ty's grandfather loved airplanes. His grandfather infected him with the flying bug.

Grandpa, I used to listen to you say something was beauty full and thought the phrase came from a lack of education. But, you were right —this is beauty full. The word beautiful just doesn't capture the magic that's here. I can almost hear you speak those words, and I feel a closeness to you and all that is here. I wish I could tell you that.

The moment passed and his thoughts turned to Blades. He filled the coffeepot and started back to the meadow, his heart lighter, and his outlook brighter.

When he passed the robins, they did not acknowledge his presence as they went about their task, and he liked that.

This is a magical place.

Cresting the last rise, he saw what was left of the fuselage, then the scar in the earth. Both looked out of place in the tranquil scene surrounding them.

This mess doesn't belong here.

When he reached the wreckage, Blades was still asleep so he leaned over and shook his shoulder.

"B, would you like some water?"

"Yeah."

Blades licked his lips, and then opened his mouth. Ty poured water into Blades mouth, some of it overflowing down the sides of his throat and into his shirt.

Blades smiled. "Feels good."

"Want more?"

Blades shook his head.

He put his hand on Blades' forehead and it felt hot.

"You're pretty warm; we better do something about that."

He took a handkerchief from his back pocket, soaked it with water, and placed it on Blades' forehead.

Blades responded with a smile. "Gee, Mom, I didn't know you cared."

"I'm not your mom. I don't have bumps in the

right places."

"How do you know my mom has bumps in the right places?"

"Hey, there are a lot of things I know that you don't.

Blades grabbed his chest. "Don't make me laugh, it hurts too much."

"Speaking of hurting, didn't that hurt when you moved your arm and leg?"

"Not really. It feels a lot better."

"I thought they were broken."

"Don't think so. They're sore, that's all."

Blades looked down at his legs stretched on the ground. "Why, do they look broken?"

"No, they look fine."

Ty ran his hands along Blades left leg and found the knee swollen, but everything else normal.

"Incredible, how's your arm?"

"Oh, it's a little sore, but OK. I think my shoulder was dislocated. It hurt when I moved it, but felt pretty good when it popped back in place."

"Amazing. I would have bet money your arm and leg were broken."

"How much money?"

"Why?"

"Well, for the right amount of money I can break them for you. Heck, for the right amount of money I can even break yours."

Ty laughed. "I think we've both suffered enough damage for a while. You need to get some rest."

"Sounds like a good idea," Blades said before slipping back into unconsciousness.

He looked at Blades, then the meadow, and felt the incongruity of being in the wrong place.

This place is special, and pain doesn't belong here. Maybe we don't belong here. Maybe we're just transients passing through to some place else. If we don't belong here, where do we belong? I sure hope you make it B.

The next three days were spent tending to Blades, making trips to the stream, and eating a diet of peanuts and pretzels. Ty found two additional coffeepots, cutting down on the number of trips for water. He made beds of grass and blankets, and Blades continued to run a high fever.

I wonder if it's only a matter of time.

CHAPTER 11

Day 37

Ty awoke to a clear blue sky with fluffy cumulus clouds.

How many times have I looked down on you? Too many to count. But today, I'm down here instead of up there. Today, I belong down here. Tomorrow I don't know where I will belong, but today I'm here. Who knows where any of us belong?

"Hey Ty, you awake."

Ty rolled over and was startled to see Blades sitting up, leaning against a piece of fuselage.

"B, you look a lot better this morning."

"I feel a lot better, as a matter of fact, I'm hungry. Do we have anything to eat?"

"Peanuts and pretzels?"

"I'll take them, I'll take anything."

Ty tossed over a bag of peanuts. Blades tore off a corner with his teeth, and then emptied the bag into his mouth.

"I'm going to need more than this," Blades said between chews.

Ty tossed over several more bags, including pretzels. Blades continued to devour the snacks as if they were culinary treats.

"Aren't you going to have some?" Blades asked as he tore open another bag.

"Naw, I'm tired of peanuts and pretzels. Let me know when you need some water."

"I need some water," Blades replied and then grinned.

Ty rolled over and groaned as he sat.

"What the heck was that? You sound like an old man."

"I am an old man."

"What are you talking about? You and I are the same age, and I'm not old."

Ty stretched his right arm, "We're both old men."

Blades body stiffened, "You may be an old man, but I'm not. Age is just a state of mind, and I can be as young as I want to be."

"Blades, you just never accepted that you've become old."

Blades threw a bag of peanuts, striking Ty's chest. "Take that back! I'm not old! I never will be!"

"Yeah, just how long has it been since young girls checked you out?"

"Young girls check me out all the time."

"They may check out the uniform, but it's been thirty years since they looked at you that way."

"No way! Young girls still check me out. Ty you were old when you were eight!"

Ty winced and his face turned red. "You mean because I was responsible while you were out sowing wild oats; because I was studying while you were out partying; because I went to church while you stayed in bed and recovered from the night before; because I'm not the screw up you are that makes me old, is that what you mean, because I'm not going to apologize for my life, I'm not going to sit here and let you criticize me for being responsible, take the log out of your own eye before you talk about the splinter in my thumb."

Blades ears turned red. "Don't quote that Bible crap to me! You're a fine one to talk, always blaming that god of yours when things don't go right instead of taking responsibility for your own actions. You do the same stupid things over and over again and when it turns out the same way you say 'Oh, I guess it just wasn't meant to be' or 'I guess it just wasn't God's will' instead of trying something new. You want to blame me, or that god of yours, or anyone else but you. Well I'm not going to apologize for the life I had, and if I had more fun than you, well that's just your fault. Don't blame me!"

Ty stood, threw the bag of peanuts back at Blades, and walked toward the stream.

"Yeah, that's right, run away you coward. You've been running away your whole life."

Ty did not feel pain or stiffness as he walked, only rage.

You sanctimonious bastard! You screw up your life and then criticize me for being successful. I should just leave you there to die you son of a bitch. You have never been a good friend. I just felt sorry for you and never had the courage to tell you I wanted you out of my life. You bastard, you sanctimonious bastard! You go to hell!

As he walked, his rage subsided to remorse and then to despair.

He's all I have. Other than Lily, he's the only one I could count on to tell me the truth, even when I didn't want to hear the truth. Maybe he's right. Maybe I do blame others. Maybe I'm jealous of his life. It was easier than mine. He never had to worry about anyone. He didn't even worry about himself.

Ty continued to walk and thought about the fight.

Why did it bother him when I said he's old? Is he afraid of dying? No, I've seen him in life and death situations and he never flinched. Was it all an act? Why is he so afraid of getting old?

Ty walked along the tree line until he came to a pawpaw tree. The diet of pretzels and peanuts had worn thin, and the sight of the golden greenish fruit lifted his spirits. He sunk his teeth into the ripe flesh that tasted like a cross between an apple and a pear, devouring the fruit in seconds. He picked another, and then another, until he could eat no more.

"This is stupid; I'm stupid, how could I let him get to me like that. How could I have said all those things? Now I have to go back and apologize to him."

Ty picked several more fruit from the tree and started walking back to the camp. The return walk seemed farther than the outbound.

"God I hate it when I do this. I hate it when I say things I have to apologize for. How could I be so stupid!"

When he arrived at the wreckage, Ty found Blades asleep, and sat down next to him, tossing one of the fruit up in the air with his right hand, and then catching it in the same hand. He watched the clouds pass overhead, then lay down, and drifted off to sleep. When he awoke, Blades was sitting next to him eating a pawpaw.

"What are these?" Blades asked as he smacked his lips.

"They're pawpaw."

"Well, they taste like maw maw to me," Blades said, then smiled.

Ty returned the smile, picked up a twig and started drawing in the earth. "Hey, Blades, I'm sorry about the things I said."

"We both said things we shouldn't have."

"Yeah, but I'm still sorry."

Ty looked in the distance and saw low-level clouds starting to form on the horizon.

"You see what I see?"

"Yep, it's going to get wet."

"Uh huh. We need to move someplace that will stay dry."

"Man, I'm not moving very far."

Blades pointed to one of the wings that lay against a small hill, forming a pocket. "If we could just get over there, under that wing."

"That's big enough for both of us."

"I think that's a great idea. The ground slopes downhill, so that rain will drain away."

Ty picked up one of the coffeepots, and walked

over to the wing, where he used the pot to scoop up dirt and pack it against the trailing edge of the wing.

"You know I could sit here and watch you work all day," Blades said.

Ty smiled as he scooped another pot of dirt. "You've been like that all your life. Remember when we got that job laying brick?"

"God, how could I forget?"

Ty stopped and looked into the western sky. "I passed some masons on my way in to work…That seems like such a long time ago, yet it's only been days."

Ty went back to packing the dirt against the wing. "I remembered those steaming cups of coffee on crisp, cold mornings. You know, I think I would have been content to be a mason. It was—"

"Not me. I would never have been happy doing that."

"I disagree. There are quite a few similarities between flying and masonry. Anyone can do either, but it requires study, practice, and artistry to do either well. I think that statement can be made about almost any occupation. The biggest difference between masonry and flying is, in masonry, you're outdoors observing the weather. In flying, you're outdoors in the weather. Both are honorable occupations that contribute to the well being of society. I think I would have been a good mason."

"Well, it wasn't for me," Blades replied. "I'm glad I didn't have to do it for a living. The mornings were cold and the afternoons hot. I liked seeing the products of my labor, but the work was hard. I'm glad my office was a comfortable, clean place, high in the sky with a fantastic view.

"Yeah, me too. It's good to know where you belong."

Ty finished packing dirt against the wing. "There, that should keep the water out."

It was mid afternoon, and thunderheads were starting to roll east across the Cumberland Plateau, toward the Tennessee Valley. Ty heard faint thunder in the distance as he used the coffeepot to scoop a trench around the wing. He found a piece of aluminum big enough for Blades, and wound strands of wire together to form a rope. He wrapped the rope around the sheet of aluminum, and then pulled the homemade sled over next to Blades. Drops of sweat fell from the tip of his nose, and a smile came across his face as he stood looking down at Blades.

Blades looked down at the sled, then up at Ty, then back down at the sled. "Very impressive, but are you certified to drive it."

"Want to go for a test spin?"

"Do I have a choice?"

"Nope."

"Didn't think so."

A bolt of lightning struck a ridge in the distance and Ty counted the seconds until he heard thunder.

"Eighteen seconds, it's about three miles away. We better get moving."

Ty helped Blades roll onto the sled. The polished aluminum bottom made pulling the sled across the grass easy, and in a few seconds, both men were at the opening to their new home. The sky turned dark, and the interval between the flashes of lightning and the claps of thunder grew shorter as Ty helped Blades roll off the sled and then went back to get the grass bedding and blankets. Just as the last bed had been made under the wing, a bolt of lightning struck the nearby ridge, and large raindrops started to fall. Ty slid his body under the wing seconds before the thunderhead opened the rain gates.

"You know, it's pretty nice in here," Blades said. "I could get used to this, although you're going to have to find someplace else. I need more space for my furniture."

"I'll see what I can work out."

Ty watched the thunderstorms pass overhead.

"God I love thunderstorms," Blades said, his face showing excitement. "They're so powerful."

"Yeah, powerful enough to knock the engine right off a wing. If it weren't for a thunderstorm, we wouldn't be here right now. I can do without them, thank you very much."

As Ty finished speaking, lightning struck a tree at the edge of the meadow, and he felt a tingle as current passed through him.

"Maybe we should find someplace else," Blades said as he moved away from the metal.

"Sounds like a good plan to me. I know when it's time to move."

When the thunderstorm passed, Ty relaxed and drifted off to sleep in the cool damp air.

CHAPTER 12

Day 36

    Ty awoke to the smell of grass, and breathed it in as if it were a drink of cool water. He felt all was right with the world, until he rolled over on his left side. The physical drama that had played out in seconds seven days earlier, was taking much longer to heal.

    "Yeeoow!"

    "Well good morning to you too," Blades said. "I trust I look better than you feel."

    Ty saw Blades standing, steadying himself with one arm on the wing.

    "How'd you get up?"

    "I needed to take a leak and thought it was time I did something for myself."

    "Are you OK?"

    "Seem to be. Ready for some maw maw?"

    Ty lay back down and pulled the blanket up over his shoulders. "Not really. The sun is just up, what are you doing out of bed? You're the one that used to hate to get up in the morning."

    "I still do, but the throbbing woke me. Seems like every part of my body moves with every heartbeat, know what I mean?"

    "Yeah, I know what you mean," Ty said as he rubbed his head. "Man I wish I had some aspirin."

    "Why would you want aspirin when we have

this?"

Ty looked up and saw Blades downing a small bottle of whiskey. Two empty bottles lay at his feet. Ty felt a combination of fear and anger. When Blades was younger, he was an entertaining drunk; now he was just mean.

"Does it help?"

"Give me a couple of minutes and I'll tell ya. Of course it helps!"

The tone in Blades voice conveyed that the word stupid had been left off the end of the sentence. He called them stupid statements; statements that should end with the word stupid or a more colorful adjective. Sentences like 'Well you can tell the judge you slept with his wife if you like, …" or "Go ahead and stick your tongue on the frozen gate pole…" or "Why don't you turn the airplane upside down to see what's in the carpets, ."

Blades held a PhD in stupid statements, and Ty had felt their blunted trauma too many times for his liking.

"Well, I'd rather have aspirin," Ty said with disgust in his voice.

"I'd rather have alcohol and aspirin," Blades responded as he reached for another bottle.

"Where'd you find that?"

"In my carryon."

"Your carryon! Where did you find your carryon?"

"Look for the hole where the fuselage dug in before it flipped over," Blades said, his words slurring together. "Our cases are behind the bushes to the right, next to the first aid box."

"First aid box! Where's the first aid box?"

Blades waved the bottle in the direction of the wreckage. "Oh yeah, I forgot to tell ya'. The first aid box is by our carryons,"

Ty scrambled out from under the wing, the pain a minor hindrance, and walked toward the fuselage until he came to the scar in the earth.

"Where did you say you saw our bags?"

"Over there, to the right, behind those bushes."

Blades waved his arm and then fell, muttering what he called social profanities.

Behind a large row of bushes, Ty found the contents of the forward galley. Strewn across the ground were cans of soda, bottled water, the first aid kit, coffee, coffeepots, tea, peanuts, pretzels and cookies. He opened the first aid kit, tore open two packets of aspirin, and downed them with one of the bottles of water. Knowing he had taken aspirin made him feel better.

As he drank the last of the water in the bottle, Ty saw something orange 150 feet away. He walked toward the object, the pain in his shoulder a distant memory. When he was closer, Ty's heart raced as he recognized the Emergency Locator Transmitter.

"The ELT! The ELT! I found the ELT! We can call out a mayday!"

Ty picked up the box, and walked back to Blades. When he rounded the end of the wing, he saw Blades sitting on the ground.

"B! I found the ELT! I found it!"

"It won't do any good," Blades said, his speech slurred.

"What do you mean it won't do any good?"

"It won't do any good," Blades repeated.

"Sure it will. It's sending out a signal."

"To who?"

"To the satellite! It goes to the satellite and to anyone else monitoring the frequency"

"And who will hear the satellite?"

"NASA! The Air Force! Anyone flying overhead!"

Blades pointed up at the sky. "Look up. Does anything strike you as peculiar?"

Ty looked up at the clear, blue sky. "No."

"It's morning. Do you see any vapor trails? There should be vapor trails by now. Do you see any?"

"But the satellite will hear…" Ty said, his voice trailing off. "It could send a signal to…"

"Ty, there's no one there."

"What the heck is that supposed to mean? There are people all around. They just haven't found us yet."

"You think so? How far did we crash from Knoxville?"

Ty slumped to a sitting position. "I don't know; four or five miles, I guess."

"And how long have we been out here?"

Ty shrugged his shoulders. "Seven or eight days."

"A large commercial airliner crashes five miles from a city of over 100,000 people, and no one comes to investigate for eight days? Come on, get real."

"But there have to be people."

Blades pointed at the ridgeline. "Do you see any houses or power lines? Do you know any ridge around Knoxville that doesn't have at least one house or tower on it somewhere?"

Ty looked up at the ridge. "Maybe we remember it wrong and we crashed in the mountains, far from anyone."

"Yeah, that would explain the lack of vapor trails and no one finding us. Come on Ty. There's no one there!"

Ty watched his dream of rescue die. He lay down, drained and exhausted, and continued to search the sky for any sign of man. He gazed into the distance and his anger began to build. He wrapped a blanket around his shoulders, climbed back under the wing, and fluffed his pillow of grass and blankets. His rage dissipated and he escaped into the solace of sleep.

Ty awoke to Blades cursing. He looked up to see Blades looking at the western horizon.

"I just got to sleep. How about cutting me a little slack."

"You've been asleep for hours, the sun's already overhead."

Ty rubbed his eyes, and looked at the shadow of the wing on the ground. When he stretched, pain shot down his left side.

"Damn."

Blades gave him a sympathetic look. "Still a little sore?"

"Yeah, just a bit."

"Me too. You know what, I need some coffee. If you'll gather some wood, I'll make the fire and brew some Jo."

"You're on. Hey, what was all the language about?"

"Aw, I forgot and leaned against my right shoulder. That, and my head hurts."

"Think it's infected?"

"No, it's not the outside of my head. Too much whiskey and not enough women."

Ty felt smug satisfaction in Blades' hangover as he started searching for firewood. He bent over and picked up sticks without pain. After a few minutes, he had collected enough wood. Blades arranged three stones in a triangle around a wad of crumpled paper. Ty put the wood between the stones and Blades lit the paper. Within minutes, a fire was established. Blades opened a pack of coffee, dumped it into the pot, filled the pot with bottled water, and put the pot on the stones placed around the fire. The coffee gave off a pleasant aroma and Ty's mouth watered as Blades poured the black liquid into two cups.

"Man, that's good," Ty said between sips.

Blades held up his cup. "You know what would

go great with this? Six eggs, a country fried steak and homemade biscuits, all covered in milk gravy."

"How about a thick slice of cheese and a loaf of fresh baked bread."

"Oh yeah. That would do too. Or how about some trout from that stream of yours?"

Ty stood, almost spilling his coffee. "Trout! That's a great idea. Why didn't I think of that?"

"'Cause you're not as smart as me."

"Give me your knife, B! I'm going to get some trout."

Ty headed across the meadow to the tree line, crossing the distance in record time. Before he knew it, he was standing at the water's edge. Using the knife, he stripped the branches from the straight shaft of a small tree, and whittled a barb on the narrow end.

His first attempts at spearing were unsuccessful. Several times, he sharpened the tip of the spear after striking a rock, but the more he missed, the more determined he became. He watched the fish in the stream rise to feed on small insects, and noticed a pattern in their swimming. They preferred to feed in swift water where food was brought to them, so he positioned himself at the inlet to a large pool. Within ten minutes, he speared a large trout. Practice improved his proficiency and within half an hour, he had speared six fish. He strung the fish on the spear and headed back, a triumphant hunter.

When Blades saw Ty emerge from the tree line, he rekindled the fire. Blades piled rocks to support a spit, passed the spear through the mouths and out the tails of two of the fish, and then laid the spear across the rocks. When the fish started to fall apart, Blades pulled off a piece with his fingers, and then dropped it.

"That's hot!"

Ty pulled a piece off the fish and blew on it as he rolled it in his fingers. When it was cool, he put the piece in his mouth and found the flavor rich and sweet. The meat dissolved on his tongue.

"Oh, that's great."

Blades pulled off a second piece, cooled it, put it in his mouth, and then nodded in agreement. The taste of the coffee enhanced the flavor of the fish, and they ate all six fish. When the last morsel was gone, Ty leaned against the fuselage, licked his fingers and sipped the last of his coffee. Before he could speak, Blades broke the silence.

"Let's go and get some more."

Ty looked at his friend. "Maybe you should stay here and collect wood, while I get more fish."

"Maybe you're right."

When Ty returned with four more fish he was surprised to see Blades sitting beside a mound of clothes, peanuts, pretzels and packets of coffee.

Blades said as he patted the pile. "This was all I could get before I gave out"

"Before you gave out? Is there more?"

"Oh, heck yeah! There's a lot more. We had several rerouted bags and some of the baggage from the scheduled run.

Blades lifted up a small package that drooped in

his hand. "Candy Bar? I found a suitcase full of junk food. The chocolate's a bit soft. Want some chips?"

Ty looked through the mound and found coats, pants, socks, underwear, cheese, sausage, canned salmon, candy bars, Twinkies, HoHo's, a box of hard Krispy Creme donuts, Moon Pies and a large smoked ham.

"I left the ladies garments," Blades said as he chewed the candy bar. "Didn't think we'd need them."

"Is there more food out there?"

"Don't know. Most of that came from two bags. There are more bags and a small metal suitcase I couldn't get open. I don't know what the little case contains. It has a good lock on it and I'm hoping it's a gun."

"Who would pack all this food?"

"I don't know," Blades replied as he stuffed a donut in his mouth, leaving a ring of powdered sugar around his lips. "But I'm willing to bet they're pretty big."

After eating the fish and some cheese, Ty settled down for a nap.

"Ty, we need to find some shelter," Blades said, interrupting Ty's attempt to drift off. "Life under a wing in a thunderstorm isn't good."

Ty nodded. "Yep. It's a lightning magnet."

Blades groaned as he stood. "Let's gather up the supplies we can use and put them under the wing. Then we can find a better place, like a cave."

Blades started dragging suitcases to the wing,

and Ty joined him. They snacked on crackers, pretzels, and potato chips as they worked, and the act of working took Ty's mind off his aches and pains.

The first piece of luggage opened contained women's makeup, shorts, and a bathing suit. Ty held up the bathing suit. "Vacation."

Blades winced. "Yep, and for a really big person."

The second bag was a hard-sided travel case that contained a shaving kit, a pair of jeans that fit Ty, and a couple of shirts. The third and fourth suitcases were businessmen's bags with shaving kits, underwear, and white shirts. The fifth bag was Blades' bonanza. It contained two pair of jeans, a pair of wool outdoor pants, and three flannel shirts. The jeans had a thirty-four waist, with thirty-four inseam.

"Eureka!" Blades said as he held up the jeans. "Exactly my size! Sorry buddy, but you're going to have to buy some new clothes."

"Eureka? What's that all about?"

"It means 'I have —.'"

"I know what it means. Do people really say that anymore?"

"I was being witty."

"Witty or jocular?"

"Oooo! A four-dollar word. I'm impressed."

Ty cocked his head to the side. "Hey, there's more here than just a pretty face."

"God, I hope so. If you think that's a pretty face you better take a closer look at your reflection."

"OK, it's an old pretty face."

"Don't go there. We've been down that path, and it wasn't pretty.

"OK, but how do you know his name is Buddy?"

Blades stopped rummaging through the clothes and looked up.

"Wouldn't you hate to be called Buddy? If someone walked up to you and said, 'How's it going Buddy?' you wouldn't know if they knew you or were just making conversation."

The sixth and seventh bags were more businessmen's bags, and one of them contained a radio. Blades scanned both the AM and FM frequencies. Aside from the occasional static pop from lightning somewhere over the horizon, there were no signals. He gave Ty a look as if to say, "I told you so."

Blades had saved the eighth suitcase for last. It was a reinforced aluminum case with sturdy combination locks.

"Too bad neither one of us worked in baggage handling I've seen them destroy bags like this with one arm tied behind their backs."

Ty held up the case and looked at the locks. "I don't know. I've seen a case like this run over with a loaded baggage cart and still not pop open."

"Well, that's because it didn't have the concentrated efforts of two seasoned pilots focused on it."

Blades picked up a piece of the landing gear.

"Guess we won't be needing this anymore. My guess is she'll never fly again."

Blades walked back and handed the instrument of destruction to Ty.

"You're in better shape than I am."

The comment shocked Ty. He had never heard Blades admit weakness, not even when beaten to a pulp.

Ty hit the first lock with a direct hit and the lock opened.

Blades face beamed. "See! Told you it couldn't take the concentrated efforts of two seasoned pilots."

With a second blow, the other lock popped open and Ty looked toward the sky.

"Please don't let it be a computer."

Blades opened the case and both men broke into laughter. They beat the ground, pointed at each other, and held their stomachs. Ty was the first to speak.

"Who would have ever guessed?"

"It figures."

The case was filled with money.

CHAPTER 13

"Somewhere there's a drug dealer that's not too happy right now," Ty said as he picked up a stack of money and flipped through it.

"Too damned bad!"

"I guess I always knew we were pawns in the drug trade. Some poor sucker risked his life to bring drugs to the U.S., and was paid less than you and I make in a week."

"Hell ,Ty, maybe it was one of our own. A flight attendant could have carried it in their bag or a mechanic may have hid it in an inspection compartment. Who knows, it's just a damn shame."

Blades face turned red as he picked up a bundle of bills. "It's a God damned perversion, that's what it is!"

"Easy, B, you are going to give yourself a heart attack."

"God damn it, Ty! The military transformed the beautiful act of flying into an instrument of death, and these God damned drug dealers used us to deliver death for profit. Drugs and war. The innocents pay the price. The money-grubbing drug dealer. The power hungry General. They both trade human misery for profit. They profane the very act of life. God damn 'em. God damn 'em to hell!"

Ty sat in stunned silence. After a few moments, he held up a bundle of bills. "You know how much money is here? Five million dollars!"

"That figures. All dressed up and nowhere to go. Well, let's split it down the middle. Half to you and half to me."

Blades scooped out half of the cash onto the ground. "Now that I'm rich, I'm going to buy you some new duds."

"Quite right," Ty said using his best English accent. "Would you like a bath, Sir?"

"Lead the way."

"Are you sure you're up to it?"

"If you take it slow, I can do it. Is there someplace along the way to rest?"

Ty smiled as he thought about the log under the cedar tree. "Boy do I have a place to show you. You're going to love it."

Ty tied two pairs of jeans, shirts, underwear and socks to the spear, and started walking toward the stream. Blades followed, but after a hundred yards had to stop and rest.

"Do you want to go back and get my cane, B?"

"It's not my legs, it's my insides. I don't think a cane will help."

"Let's turn around and try it again tomorrow."

"Sounds like a good plan to me. How about helping me get back on my feet."

Blades walked back to camp without stopping, and collapsed in front of the wing.

"Are you OK?"

"I just need a little rest."

Blades slept the rest of the day, waking once for a drink.

As the sun went down, Ty watched the light fade while Blades snored behind him.

"God I hate the night."

CHAPTER 14

Day 35

Ty awoke before sunrise, and saw Blades sitting by a fire.

"You OK, B?"

"Yeah. When I was walking back yesterday, something inside my gut tore, but I feel a lot better this morning."

"You sure?"

"Yeah, go figure. I want to go down to that stream today. I'm getting tired of smelling like chicken soup."

"Well, Mr. Chicken Soup, how about some smoked ham for breakfast?"

"It's already on, and the coffee's almost at a boil."

Ty crawled out from under the wing to warm by the fire.

"Hey, you do smell like chicken soup."

Blades smiled. "Make you hungry?"

"No."

"Good. I don't want you to go cannibal like those guys that crashed in the Andes."

"I don't think you have anything to worry about. Those guys didn't have any choice, and we have plenty of food."

After eating breakfast, Ty relaxed next to the

fire until mid morning when they started walking to the stream. Blades stopped several times to rest, each stop a bit longer than the previous.

"Where's that special spot you told me about?" Blades said as he sat down for another rest.

"It's right through those bushes, but you'll need to be well rested because there's nowhere to sit down until we get there. It's about twice as far as you have walked between the last few stops."

Blades lay back on the grass and looked up at the sky. "I sure wish I were up there."

Ty looked up at the sky, and then sat down next to Blades. "Me too, but we're not. Maybe someday."

"I doubt that. I think our flying days are finished. Unless they give you wings."

Ty frowned.

After several minutes, Blades stood. "OK, I'm ready. Let's go to this great place."

Ty smiled and pointed to a trail that entered a thicket of rhododendron bushes. "Through there. The first time I came this way, I pushed my way through the bushes, but I wised up and started following this deer trail. You lead."

Blades followed the trail into the thicket and walked through the bushes. After several minutes the bushes starting to thin and they stepped out into the clearing with the log and cedar tree.

"Over there," Ty said as he pointed to the log.

Blades walked over to the log and collapsed.

"Oh, this is great. I think I'll just stay here

while you go on."

"No way! The best is yet to come."

Fifteen minutes later Blades was ready to continue. When he came out of the bushes next to the stream, he stopped and looked at the tranquil setting.

"You were right. This is a great place. No wonder you come here a lot."

"I thought you would like it. All my troubles seem to disappear when I'm down here."

Ty removed his clothes and slid into the water, while Blades rested on the bank, dangling his feet in the water.

The cool water caused Ty's shoulder to ache but as he moved his arm back and forth, the pain subsided. "Come on in, B, the water's fine."

"Yeah, I've heard that before."

Blades removed his clothes and inched his way into the stream, the water flowing past him turning a murky brown.

"That's blood, isn't it?" Ty said.

Blades smiled. "Maybe. Maybe not. Of course it's blood."

"Good. I just wanted to make sure."

After several minutes, Ty felt rejuvenated, climbed out of the stream and lay on a large boulder. The boulder warmed his back and the sun warmed the rest of his body. "Doesn't get much better than this, does it B?"

"It's OK. I'm getting pretty stiff, I need to get out."

Ty leaned over to give Blades a hand and noticed he was shivering. "B, are you OK?"

"Yeah, I'm OK. I guess I should have gotten out sooner."

Ty helped Blades up on the rock, and then dried him with one of the clean shirts. By the time Ty finished dressing, Blades had stopped shivering, but he was still pale.

"Feeling better, B?"

"Yeah, I'm OK. How about tossing me some clothes."

The trip back to camp took longer than the journey outbound. Blades needed more, and longer, rest stops. When they returned to the camp, Blades slid into his bed without speaking.

It was two days before Blades was strong enough to travel to the stream, and a week before he could make the trip without stopping.

CHAPTER 15

Day 28

Ty woke to the smell of ham and coffee. He rolled over to see Blades stirring the fire with a piece of aluminum.

"Doesn't that get hot?"

Blades turned and smiled. "Well howdy do to you too, cranky."

"I am not cranky! It just seems to me that a piece of aluminum would conduct a lot of heat if you put it in a fire."

"Well, I suppose it would if you left it in for a long time."

Blades pulled the metal from the fire and swung it around in front of Ty. "Here, feel it and tell me if it's hot."

Ty shrunk back. "No thanks, I'll take your word for it."

"See, it's not that hot," Blades said as he slipped his hand over the business end of the metal, and then dropped it. "Yikes! That's hotter than I expected!"

"What were you thinking? You just pulled it from the fire."

"I know, but I thought it would cool down faster than it did."

Blades face broke into a grin.

"Guess it didn't work like I planned. I sure

didn't know that would happen."

"What's with you, Blades? You hate getting up in the morning."

"I know. It's just that there is something about this place that makes me want to get up and see what is out there."

"Why weren't you that way yesterday?"

"I don't know. I used to wake up and think, 'Why am I getting up at O'dark thirty when any idiot knows we're not supposed to be up before the sun.' I would lie in bed and curse those accounting idiots that made up the operations schedule, and vow to someday tell them to stick it where the sun doesn't shine. The irony that I was where the sun didn't shine wasn't lost on me, and sometimes I got a good chuckle out of it. Hey, you know what? I think today's the day."

Blades turned his face toward the sky. "Hey! Stick it where the sun doesn't shine!"

Ty climbed out into the cool morning air. "You are really in a good mood."

"You bet! Today's the day."

"The day for what?"

"Today's the day to find out what is out there. Today is moving day."

Ty picked up the coffeepot and poured some of the black liquid into a cup. "You think you are up to it?"

"Yep. If I am not now, I never will be. It is time for us to get moving, and I even made some red eye gravy to start the day off right."

Ty looked at the dark liquid bubbling in the homemade pan fashioned out of a piece of aluminum.

"What the heck is this stuff?"

"Oh, it is great stuff. You just pour coffee in with the drippings left from frying the ham and cook it down just as you cook down maple syrup. It's some of the best eating you will ever find."

Ty was raised on a cattle ranch where he was taught to look down on pork. He remembered his grandfather telling him, "They're filthy animals. Even the Bible says not to eat them. The Bible says we are supposed to eat beef."

Ty wondered how much of his grandfathers attitude was based on the Bible, and how much was based on the economics of supply and demand of the cattle market. He watched Blades immerse the slices of ham into the thick brown liquid.

"It does smell good," Ty said as he reached for a fork.

Blades motioned for Ty to try a piece. Ty used the fork to break a piece from one of the slices of ham lying in the dark fluid. He lifted it out, blew on it, and then placed it in his mouth. The combination of coffee and ham tasted better than he expected, and he nodded his head in approval.

"See, I told you it was good," Blades said with a look of satisfaction.

"You were right," Ty said between chews. "This is delicious. The smoky flavor mixed with the coffee gives it a whole new taste."

After eating breakfast, Ty helped Blades put a supply of pretzels, peanuts, smoked ham, and canned salmon in blankets. They rolled the blankets into bedrolls, and then bound them with strands of wire tied around them. Ty put wire through the center of the rolls to form slings, and then placed everything that was remaining under the wing.

Blades laid a piece of aluminum over the opening. "Leaving the coffee here will give us a reason to come back for the rest of the stuff."

"We might be back sooner than you think," Ty replied.

"You're such a pessimist."

Ty placed an open hand on his chest. "I like to think of myself as a realist."

"Realist. The pessimist's word for pessimist."

"I am not a pessimist!"

"That is not the way I see it."

"Well, you see it wrong!"

Blades picked up his bedroll and placed the sling around his neck, the blanket resting on his back. Ty placed the sling around his neck, but with the bedroll in front, using it as a sling to cradle his arm, his teeth clinched as he watched Blades turn towards the east.

You sanctimonious bastard! You have no right to talk to me like that. Who do you think you are? I wish your scalp would come loose and fall right off your head!

The vision of Blades hair falling backwards like a cheap toupee brought a quick smile to his lips, followed by a short laugh.

"What is so funny?" Blades said as he stopped and turned around.

"Oh, nothing. I was just remembering a funny story; I will have to tell you about it some time."

Blades shook his head, then resumed walking.

As they entered the tree line, Ty stopped to look back at what had become home.

"I wonder if we will ever see her again."

A deer trail ran parallel to the water, and they followed it downstream in search of bigger water. The stream became larger as other streams joined it. When the sun was half an hour above the horizon, a sound lifted Ty's spirit. The faint sound of hope developed into promise, and the promise into excitement. The excitement increased as the distant roar became louder.

The sound of falling water quickened their step, and they came to a gorge where the stream disappeared over the edge. The sound of water falling into a pool echoed off the other side of the gorge. Walking along the rim of the gorge, Ty caught glimpses of a river below. Trees along the bank shielded the river from view.

The deer trails down the hillside were steep, and Ty held on to rhododendron bushes for support mist from the waterfall made the ground slippery. The air titillated with spray and a clean smell, until a waterfall leapt from the hillside.

Blades face mirrored awe. "Would you look at that!"

"Wow."

Ty absorbed his surroundings.

"I feel like I am in a picture," Ty said.

The awesome power of falling water anchored him where he was, yet beckoned him forward. The engulfing beauty both mesmerized and paralyzed.

"Have you ever seen anything so perfect?" Blades said.

Ty did not reply as he focused on the falling water, the fish swimming, and the roar. The roar engulfed everything in a blanket of power that seemed also to offer protection.

"I think we've found our home for the night," Blades shouted, his voice drawn into the roar.

Ty looked at Blades and saw a child, long ago disappeared, emerge from the sentence of adulthood. Blades face was a mixture of wonder, excitement and joy; a perfect picture of enthusiasm for life.

"B, this is a wonderful spot, but I think it will be pretty cold sleeping here. How about we spend the night downstream, out of the mist?"

The child's face disappeared, replaced by that of a sensible adult, the smile still there, but subdued. Ty's heart sank as he saw the enthusiasm wane and the child relegated back to the prison of adulthood.

"Yeah, you are right," Blades replied, "But I want to stay where we can still see it."

The innocent smile of the child reemerged in full force.

Ty smiled and nodded his head in agreement.

Blades looked back at the waterfall every few

seconds as they walked downstream. Ty had never seen the child in Blades. It was part of his persona he kept hidden.

Ty collected rhododendron branches and Blades stripped small saplings to construct a lean-to. It was almost dark when the shelter was finished and they settled in for the night. The leaves provided soft bedding and the blankets warmth. A full moon emerged over the mountain, dusting everything in gold.

"I could live here forever," Blades said as he looked up at the stars.

Ty did not know if Blades was talking to him, the mountains, the sky or all three. It did not make any difference; Blades was happy in the moment and that made it perfect. The trials of tomorrow would come soon enough.

The falling water pounded the earth, massaging Ty's body, and cradling his spirit. He smiled as he drifted off to sleep.

CHAPTER 16

Day 27

Ty awoke and looked up at a clear blue sky. The night of sleep had refreshed more than just his body. His mind was alert, and he felt exhilarated at the prospects of a new day. Thirst made the water inviting, and he knelt down, placing his face in the clear water. The water caressed his face, and embraced him with a kiss. He drank in the cool, sweet kiss, the liquid flowing over his tongue and down his throat. The water satisfied his thirst, and something deeper. A need to be. A need to know. A need to experience.

Ty pulled his face from the water and allowed the excess to fall back into the flowing stream. To wipe his face seemed sacrilege. The water dripped from his entire face, then from his chin, and the last drop returned from the tip of his nose. His action was not of necessity, but of reverence; an act of love of all that supported him. Ty felt one with the world, a feeling he had not experienced since childhood.

"I wonder how I could have forgotten what this feels like.

Ty thought about the hours spent in a church pew. The promises of fulfillment never produced such clarity of being. Noise and clutter over the course of his life had drowned out the act of being. He recognized moments missed and moments refused; moments of passion that brought him so close, yet went ungrasped. He became filled with a mixture of regret, awe and excitement. When he looked at the water, it looked back. For the first time in his life, Ty saw water.

Blades shout broke the trance. He stood chest deep in the pool below the falls, a trout in each hand. Teeth and lips formed a smile that obliterated his face as he shook the fish, their tails flapping. Ty realized he had everything; food, water, shelter, and companionship. Everything but his family, and his viewpoint of life was forever changed.

But, childhood truths die hard, and the moment of clarity slipped away, replaced by the cloudiness taught by parents, teachers and mentors. Cloudiness taught to parents by their parents, a veil of ignorance passed from generation to generation that tarnishes even the brightest moments of life. A veil passed on not in spite, but in love. The veil of ignorance blankets everything; smothering potential and inciting wars. In rare moments of clarity, the veil is lifted and the brilliant colors of life are revealed. Nevertheless, the veil is self-healing, and mends tears in its fabric until clarity is obscured and the old view is restored. The veil dulls the memory of moments of clarity, but cannot erase them completely. When the veil is torn, it is forever weakened. The once flawless view of the veil is marred by a scar.

The veil of ignorance covered Ty once again and he returned to seeing life in the "old" way, but deep in his being was the remembrance of the moment of clarity; deep in his being was the seed of knowledge of a different being. A deep longing grew in him, a longing that required fulfillment.

Blades walked out of the pool with the fish. "Look at these."

"I want to find my house!" Ty said.

"You what?" Blades replied with a surprised look.

"I want to find my house."

Blades lowered his hands holding the trout. "But we just found this place, and I am tired. I need a rest."

"I know, but I want to find my house."

"Is it that important?"

Ty looked down to prevent Blades from seeing his eyes. "Yeah, it is that important."

Blades let out a long breath, "OK, but how about getting a good night's rest before we go?"

Ty pretended to sneeze, and then wiped his eyes with his shirtsleeve. "Thanks. You are right, we need to rest. We can go the day after tomorrow."

"Sounds good to me. That will give us time to go back to the plane for more clothes. Autumn is coming, and who knows how long it will be before we are back here."

Blades gutted the fish and laid them on a rock at the side of the stream before making another fire ring. Ty collected twigs and branches to start a fire and within minutes, his mouth watered as the smell of trout cooking filled the air.

Blades grew stronger with the passage of every day, but it was a week before they returned to the plane.

CHAPTER 17

Day 20

Both men were stronger than when they left the plane, and the walk back took three hours. As Ty emerged from the tree line, he saw the tail of the airplane pointing toward the sky, a memorial to all that had been.

"Wow. What a difference a few days makes" Ty said. "It only took us three hours to get back here, and that included climbing up the ridge."

As they approached, he saw Blades wipe his eyes.

"What's the matter?"

Blades stopped and looked up at the sky, a glistening still visible in his eyes. "I was remembering what it felt like to push the rudder pedal, turn the wheel and make the world spin. God, I wish I could do that just one more time."

A lump formed in Ty's throat and he could not speak. He felt the same calling; it was his old self, calling him back to what had been; to what he could have been. The call was strong, and he felt sad knowing it would never be. His old self had started to fade into oblivion; a distant memory becoming more transparent with the passing of every day.

When he reached the wreckage, he pretended to go about business as usual, gathering items and making small talk. When he thought Blades was not looking, he ran his hand over the leading edge of the wing and remembered the majestic airplane sitting on the tarmac; her skin smooth and shiny, polished by the rush of thousands of hours of air passing over the metal.

Blades went through the luggage again, picking out clothes that would keep them warm. It was a silent ritual, as if he was on holy ground. He found a bag with shoulder straps that allowed it to be worn like a backpack and started filling the bag with clothes, peanuts, pretzels, and packs of coffee. The rest of the luggage and food he stored under the wing.

Blades tried to put the bag on his back, but his right shoulder could not support the weight. He slipped his walking stick through the shoulder straps, and then stuffed blankets in the space between the stick and the bag.

Ty gazed into the distance, trying to maintain his composure and not look at the wreckage. Grass covered parts of the plane, as the earth began wiping the scar from its face.

It was hard to let go of what might have been, and embark on what will be. The past was known, but the future was unknown, and there was no guarantee it would be better, just different.

Ty remembered what his grandfather told him, "Man is not built on what he was, but on what he may become. The foundation of man is hope and dreams, and the true enemy is hopelessness. Without hope man becomes as stagnant as concrete."

Blades handed Ty two blankets. "Put these on your shoulder to cushion the load."

Ty folded the blankets and placed them on his right shoulder, then picked up one end of the stick while Blades hoisted the other end onto his left shoulder.

At the tree line, they stopped and looked one last time.

"Goodbye Girl," Blades said softly.

Ty followed behind Blades, tears streaming down his face. He did not grieve the loss of the airplane, or their situation, but the loss of what could have been. He mourned the death of dreams, and his tears were liquid regret, anger, and fear. He wanted to curse, but was afraid to curse whom he felt was responsible, because he knew it could be himself. He felt lower than he had ever felt in his life.

They stopped for the night at the waterfall. It had become a ritual for Blades to hike to the top of the waterfall to watch the sun set. He stayed longer than usual and did not return until well after dark.

"Good sunset?" Ty asked.

"They are all good. Do you miss seeing the sun set from the cockpit?"

"I never liked flying at night."

Blades looked off into the night sky. "That was the best time for me."

Ty lay in his bed looking at the night sky before drifting off to sleep. He dreamed of finding his house with a fire in the fireplace and a pot of split pea soup on the stove. His mouth watered, and he licked his lips as he dreamt.

CHAPTER 18

Day 19

Predawn light was creeping across the sky when Ty awoke. He was the first up and the chill of the morning was heavy as he built the fire. Blades woke to the smell of fish cooking and hot coffee.

"Whoa! This is a change."

"I couldn't sleep. I'm excited about going home." Ty looked off into the distance. "I wonder what will be there."

As he ate breakfast, Ty thought about what he missed from home.

"I miss knowing that my house and wife would be there when I came home in the evening. I miss Saturday breakfast at the Strawberry Plains Café. I miss petting my dog Willie, watching Bald Eagles soar, and hearing Canada Geese overhead. I miss the smell of that old carpet I promised to replace in the bedroom. God, there are so many things I miss."

Blades did not say anything as he stirred the coals of the fire with a stick.

"Do you miss anything, B?"

"Yeah, I miss flying."

"Nothing else?"

"Nope."

" Not even people?"

Blades pulled the end of the stick out of the fire and blew on the glowing tip. "Maybe a hotdog smothered in chili and covered with onions."

"That is it?"

"A T bone steak and baked potato would be good."

"You only miss food?"

"Pretty much."

Ty stared at Blades as he thought about how much there was about Blades he did not know.

Blades broke the silence. "What do you want to take with us?

"How about some coffee."

Blades put five packs of coffee, the coffeepot, and blankets in the backpack, then slid his left arm through one of the straps and lifted the bag onto his back.

"Are you sure you can handle that? Is your shoulder OK?"

"Yeah, it's fine as long as I don't put too much weight on it. I am getting better every day."

They started walking as the sun lit the treetops on the ridge above them. The stream emptied into a riverbed that was small and shallow during summer months. Like the creek, the river passed though pools of clear water. The pools in the river were much larger than the pools in the creek, and invited swimming.

After several hours, they came to a large pool of water so clear it was difficult to judge the depth of the water. The sun had risen to almost overhead, causing the temperature to seem much hotter than it was.

Blades stripped off his clothes and dove into the water, his body sliding under the surface like a giant fish. When his head surfaced, a loud "Yeehaw!" shattered the silence.

Ty slid into the water and watched fish scatter as he swam through the coolness. He surfaced and saw Blades' feet kicking water in all directions at the other end of the pool.

"What in the world?"

The shell of a turtle surfaced with Blades hands on both sides. The turtle's legs thrashed and its head swung from side to side as it tried to bite.

"I think we have lunch," Blades shouted.

Blades swam to the edge of the pool and lifted the turtle out of the water, its head still flailing. The turtle broke free, but Blades managed to grab the shell and regain his grip.

"Get my knife," Blades shouted. "Sorry, old fella, but this is the way it has to be. You are going to give us the strength to go on."

Within seconds, the struggle was over.

Ty gathered wood for a fire while Blades made an oven pit out of rocks. They built a fire in the pit to heat the rocks, and when the fire was almost out, they put the turtle in the oven on its back.

The meat was sweet and juicy, a pleasant change from the diet of fish and berries. When he finished eating, Ty stretched out under a large Hickory tree and slipped into an afternoon nap. After an hour, the lethargy of the afternoon passed.

"Want to spend the night here or move on?" Blades said.

Blades was always more than ready to stop for the night. Every new place had territory to explore and secrets to discover.

"No, let's keep going. We still have four or five hours of daylight."

An hour before sunset they came to a section in the river with a white sand beach that sparkled in the rays of the setting sun. Ty looked at Blades and knew this was the spot for the night.

Ty was not hungry and spent the evening playing in the water and lying on the beach. Blades explored the surrounding area.

When it turned dark, Ty spread his blankets on the sand and drifted off to sleep. He dreamed of seeing the beach from far away.

CHAPTER 19

Day 18

Hunger began to gnaw at Ty as darkness turned to morning twilight. Morning dew covered the ground and he chose warmth over food. A man can go days without food, but only hours without warmth.

The arrival of the morning sun started to drive the chill back to the province of night. Blades was the first to speak.

"You hungry?"

"Yep."

Blades pulled the blanket tighter around him. "Me too. What do you think we should do?"

"It's too cold to go fishing and too wet to light a fire."

"Peanuts and coffee?"

"How are we going to make the coffee?"

"Good point. How about just peanuts?"

Ty pulled the blanket over his head. "Fine by me, but it's too cold to get up."

"Yep, winter is coming. I hate the cold."

After twenty minutes, the combination of warming air and increasing hunger caused Ty to throw off his blankets.

As they warmed in the morning sun, Ty remembered seeing the beach from far away in his dream. The dream was not haunting, but a lingering remembrance.

"I can't help but feel like I've been here," Ty said.

"Why?"

Ty looked around. "I don't know. It just feels familiar. I will remember. I just have to give it some time."

Blades packed everything back into the bag, and hoisted the bag up on his back. "You know, this is going to feel heavy tomorrow."

"Muscles are always the sorest on the second or third day. If it hurts a little today, it is going to hurt a lot tomorrow."

Blades turned and grinned. "That is why I get paid the big bucks."

They walked until they came to the crest of a ridge, where Ty stopped and turned to look back at the beach. Blades laid the bag next to the trail to rest his shoulder.

Waves of excitement flushed through Ty as memories of seeing the beach returned.

"I know where I've seen it! I saw that beach a thousand times as I drove to work. It would come into view as I crossed the bridge on the way to the airport! I remember looking at the white sand and dream of lying on it during a hot summer afternoon. I always planned to visit the beach, but never did. Son of a gun! That is where I have seen it!"

Ty laughed and slapped his thigh, causing Blades to laugh.

"There should be a bridge right up there," Ty

said as he pointed upriver. "Let's go!"

Blades shook his head and picked up the backpack as Ty started to walk.

"Whoa, pardner. Let me get this thing on my shoulder first."

After an hour, Ty came to the crest of another ridge where he stopped to let Blades catch up. When Blades arrived, he was panting. He put the bag down, and then shook his arms.

Ty looked up and down the river. There was no bridge, or any other sign of civilization. He saw river, rocks, trees and sky; but nothing made by man.

Blades turned his head from side to side to stretch his neck muscles. "How far did you say it was to the bridge?"

"Half to three quarters of a mile."

"We have walked a lot farther than that. I did not see any sign of a bridge, did you?"

"I just don't understand—What is going on? Where is it? It doesn't make—I just don't—What the hell is going on? Where is everybody? Why can't we find anything? I just don't under…"

Ty's voice trailed off as he sat down on his haunches. After a few seconds, he stood up and looked up and down the river again. When he sat back down, Ty's gaze fixated on the ground.

"I just don't understand."

After a few minutes Blades spoke. "Where do you think we are?"

"What?" Ty said as he looked up at Blades.

"Where do you think we are?"

"What do you mean? I don't understand what you mean."

"I mean, where do you think we are?"

"Look Blades I don't know what kind of game you are playing but I am not in a mood to be messed with!"

"I am not messing with you, I am just trying to get you to think about our situation."

Ty cast a of look of disdain at Blades, but the look seemed to calm Blades even more.

"Does it seem odd to you when we were flying we did not see Knoxville, or any sign of a city? There was no trace of the World's Fair Ball or anything else. Nothing. No highways, no cities, no houses. Nothing. They were all gone."

Ty's emotionless gaze fixed on Blades face, much as a student's gaze fixes on that of a master.

"It is as if we are in a time before man came to East Tennessee. Or a time long after man is gone."

Ty continued to stare at Blades.

"Does this make sense to you?" Blades said.

Ty continued to stare at Blades, then turned his gaze to the ground and sat motionless.

"Ty, are you OK?"

Ty picked up a stick and started drawing circles in the Earth. "Yeah, I'm OK. It takes time to get used to the idea that everything I love is either long dead or has never been. My wife, my children, my grandchildren — long gone or never been."

Ty continued to draw in the earth for a few minutes then stood up and looked at the horizon.

"Well, I am going to find out which it is. Dead, or not yet living. My house is a few miles upriver and I dug that basement by hand. It is either there or it is not there, and I am going to find out which it is. Daylight is burning, let's get going."

Blades picked up the backpack and followed Ty's stiff legged, defiant steps. After several minutes, Ty's gait returned to normal and they followed the path until the sun was overhead.

"I think we should stop for a rest," Blades said between breaths. "We have been going since morning without food or water. It is time to take a rest."

"It is a few hours further to my house. We can make it by nightfall."

Blades pointed toward the western horizon. "Look at the cold front moving in. The thunderheads are already starting to form over the Cumberland Plateau, and it will be an hour or so before they are here."

Ty looked to the west and saw the mountain range of clouds approaching. "OK, I know where there is a cave not too far from here. We should be able to make it before the rain gets here."

Ty resumed walking along the trail, keeping an eye on the approaching clouds. Fueled by the afternoon sun, the thunderheads began to grow and the conditions were right for them to grow into a squall line. As the storms approached, Ty heard the thunder grow louder, and picked up the pace. When he felt the cold air that precedes a downpour, he started running. Large raindrops fell as they reached

105

the entrance to the cave.

"Just in time," Blades said as he laughed.

"What? You thought I did not know where I was going?"

Ty looked at the walls of the cave. "It is said the hills of Tennessee are hollow, but this cave is different. The river carved out this cave."

The cave was twenty feet above the level of the river. It had been carved out in times of much higher water, and went back into the rock ten feet, providing excellent protection from the downpour. Ty looked at the cave and could not remember if it was bigger or smaller than he imagined. He had never been in the cave, but had seen it from a distance.

Bolts of lightning struck the hilltops around them, and claps of thunder echoed off hills and ridges. The majesty, sheer power, and potential for disaster commanded Ty's attention.

"God I loved watching these from the perch," Blades said. The perch was his name for the cockpit in flight.

Ty shook his head. "I hated them. They scared the daylights out of me."

Blades looked out at the rain pouring down. "Yeah, that's what's so great about them. You could see them boiling, the air rising thousands of feet a minute. God I miss that sight."

"Not me. I would rather be on the ground watching them. As long as I am in here, they will not hurt me. Up there they can tear my wings off like a kid with a fly."

Blades turned and looked at Ty. "What kind of kids did you hang out with?"

"You know what I mean," Ty said, his voice trailing off in a laugh. "They are just so powerful. Man wasn't made to fly through them."

The thunderstorms lasted for three hours and left the air cool and humid. The storms also left the river two feet higher, as the deluge of water washed down the hills and into the creeks, the creeks feeding the streams and the streams the river. What was once massive energy rumbling across the face of the earth was now liquid energy rushing back to the sea. Everything that had fallen to the east of them was going to pass by their doorstep. The river was too high, and the current too fast, to fish.

Ty opened the backpack. "Looks like another meal of peanuts."

"Not me, Blades replied. We passed a blackberry patch on our dash in here and I am going back there. I can almost taste them."

The berry patch was a five-minute walk from the cave, and the berries were black and sweet. After eating as many berries as he wanted, Blades sat on a rock. He saw a tree down close to the river's edge.

"Look at that!" Blades said as he pointed at the tree. "A pear tree."

"That's not a pear tree," Ty said. "That's PawPaw."

The tree was loaded with ripe, yellowish green fruit, some of which had already fallen. Both men ate until they could not eat anymore. After resting under the tree for a few minutes, they walked back to the cave.

The haze of day evaporated to the clarity of night, and soon the sky was a gathering of twinkling lights. Without a moon, the stars had a chance to shine in their own splendor. The air was warm, but the rock walls of the cave provided natural air conditioning, and the sandy floor was a comfortable bed. Ty spread his blankets on the sand and remembered the day from a much different viewpoint than at the start.

CHAPTER 20

Day 17

Birds greeted the dawn; each with their own sound, their own song. At times, it sounded like an orchestra tuning up. At times, like a hundred crossed telephone lines.

The morning was warm, and a soft wind blew down the riverbed. Ty was the first to awake, anxious to move on. His defiance of yesterday was replaced by a curiosity he needed to satisfy. He wanted to fill the void of not knowing, Not knowing if what Blades said was true. Not knowing if anyone he loved was left. Not knowing what was, what had been, or what was to come.

He shook Blades.

"Come on B."

Blades did not move.

"Come on B, daylight is burning."

"I'm awake," Blades responded with a coarse and groggy voice.

After a few minutes, Blades sat up and looked out at the river, his gaze a blank stare. Blades was more of a late night finisher than an early morning riser.

"What time did you go to sleep last night?" Ty asked.

"Same time as you. Why?"

"How come you're so groggy this morning?"

Blades looked at Ty through half open eyes. "Who says I'm groggy? I think I'm just peachy keen. You want dancing girls, go to a club."

Ty looked at him and laughed. In the military, no one was responsible for their actions the first four or five seconds after awakening, but for Blades, the time had been extended to minutes. Blades did not awake from sleep, he emerged. Ty was jealous of the deep sleep Blades enjoyed, because for him the night was an alternating series of sleep and waking, and he longed for the deep sleep of youth.

"What's for breakfast?" Blades said, a blanket still wrapped around his shoulders.

"We'll eat on the way. It will give us a chance to look for something different."

Blades stretched and then put the blankets back into the bag. He staggered to his feet, lifted the bag to his back, and stepped out onto to the trail. Ty started walking and Blades slowly followed.

The pace was slow as Blades' joints loosened, but after a couple of minutes he felt better and started pushing Ty to move faster. The trail was level and Ty was able to walk at a brisk pace. As they crested a small incline, Ty saw the purple berries of a mulberry tree at the side of the trail.

"Breakfast dead ahead."

The berries looked like blackberries, but longer with a purple cast. Deer, or anything else that could reach the berries, had already eaten everything below seven feet. The higher berries were within the reach of Blades, but just out of the reach of Ty. Blades picked two clusters of berries, giving one to Ty and keeping one. The berries melted in Ty's mouth, a cascade of thick, sweet juice covered his tongue and slipped down his throat. Blades let out a moan of contentment. After eating several clusters, Blades turned to Ty holding up a large cluster of berries.

"It doesn't get any better than this!"

Ty let out a laugh, covering his mouth with his hand. Blades teeth and lips were stained a deep purple. He pointed at Blades, while trying to keep from laughing and choking at the same time. Tears filled his eyes, and purple juice shot out his nose.

The sight of purple juice shooting out Ty's nose caused Blades to laugh, and he smiled at Ty to egg him on. More juice shot out Ty's nose. Blades fell to the ground in laughter. Ty's face and hands were covered in a hemorrhage of purple.

It took several minutes before they could control themselves. When Ty spoke, Blades laughed at his purple teeth and Ty laughed at the sight of Blades. Both men were lost in the moment, with no regards to their surroundings, the past, or the future. The moment brought an air of giddiness, and after a moment of calm, they both felt invigorated.

"Let's go!" Blades said, picking up the backpack. He walked along the trail at a fast pace, and after an hour came to a bend in the river.

Ty pointed to the other side of the river. "This is it! My house is right over there. That's the Hickory tree on my place! My house is just up that hollow!"

Ty continued to walk until he was across from the large Hickory tree. "That's it! That's it! I can't see the house, but that's it."

The river level had dropped from the night

before, and Ty waded into the water. Blades followed, holding the bag above his head. The river was shallow enough for Blades to walk across, but Ty had to swim part of the way. Ty was the first to reach the other side, where he scrambled up the bank and disappeared into the brush.

A small creek ran down the left side of the hollow. Blades followed a deer trail that paralleled the creek, until he came to a clearing. Ty was sitting on a rock with his back to Blades.

"What do you think?" Blades asked.

"I don't know. The pecan and walnut trees aren't here. There are no barns or fencing, and this rock is where my house sat."

He pointed to a depression in the ground. "This is where I dug the basement. I don't know if this is the basement filled in with dirt, or if this is what it was before I dug the hole. I don't know, I just don't know."

Ty put his face in his hands. Blades turned and walked back to the river.

Ty felt lower than he thought a human being could feel; even lower than when he left the plane. He felt lost and without hope. Dreams die hard, and his had been shattered. It is the loss of dreams that makes the death of children tragic, and the life of the elderly hopeless.

Blades sat on the bank and watched the river. After a few hours, Ty emerged from the brush, looking older and tired.

"Ty, we could stay here. I could build us a cabin and—"

"No! This is a place of the dead. It is part of my past, not my future. It's time to move on. Time to look at what will be, not what has been. Let's go."

He stood up and waded into the river as Blades hoisted the backpack above his head and followed. When they reached the other side, Ty turned and started walking down river.

"Don't you want to see what's upriver?" Blades asked.

"No. I just want to go home."

"OK, let's go home. But where would that be?"

CHAPTER 21

Blades thought what a strange concept home seemed to be. He felt wherever he was became home, and the waterfall was as good a home as any. He knew Ty did not share his feelings, and sensed that trouble was brewing. During the journey upriver, Ty was filled with hopes and dreams, but now Blades saw anger fermenting, and Ty's mood had turned foul. From past experience, Blades knew to give Ty a wide berth when he was stewing.

Blades felt the word stewing fit Ty well. When Ty was upset, he was like a boiling caldron. Unlike Blades, whose anger erupted and subsided fast, Ty's temper took a long time to come to a boil, and an even longer time to cool. During Ty's periods of ill temper, Blades knew it best to leave Ty to his own thoughts. To enter into Ty's realm was to invite retribution.

When they reached the mulberry tree, Blades' back started to hurt and he decided it was time to break the silence.

"Hey! How about stopping for some more mulberries?"

Ty did not acknowledge Blades and continued walking. Blades dropped the pack beside the trail and massaged his tired shoulders.

"You were right, it does hurt more today than it did yesterday," he yelled as Ty disappeared over the ridge ahead.

The shade of the tree felt good, and Blades ate more of the purple berries. The mulberries tasted sweet, but not as sweet as when he and Ty were laughing at each other. After resting, Blades put his left arm through the shoulder strap and hoisted the pack onto his back. A tinge of pain in his lower back told him trouble had arrived. As Blades walked down the trail, the muscles in his lower back started to cramp and then went into spasm. He pushed the pain out of his mind and continued walking, arriving at the cave just as his back went into full spasm and the pain became unbearable.

Sitting down in the cave entrance, he leaned back on the pack, pulled his arms from the shoulder straps, and lay down in the sand. Without the weight of the pack, the muscles went into stronger spasms, but the cool sand helped relieve the pain.

"I wish I would have packed some aspirin."

Blades expected Ty to be at the cave, but there was no sign Ty had stopped. He struggled to his feet, made his way down to the river, took off his clothes, and slipped into the cool water. He looked up at the pale blue sky and thought about all the times he had looked down on this river as the water massaged his back and eased the pain.

"Who ever thought it would end like this. All the scrapes and accidents I've been though, and I'm going to die an old man in bed."

Blades laughed. "Ty, you were right, we are old men, and I just never wanted to admit it. I never wanted any of this to end."

After an hour, the combination of the setting sun and cool water caused Blades to shiver. He climbed out and lay on a rock that still held the warmth of the sun until he was dry. He dressed and climbed back up to the cave where he made a bed with the blankets.

"Ty, wherever you are, I hope you are warm tonight."

Blades looked down river one more time for signs of a fire before lying down and drifting off to sleep.

CHAPTER 22

Day 16

Blades awoke before dawn and the pain in his back had subsided to a minor ache. The pangs of hunger in his stomach were strong and he remembered the pawpaw tree minutes from the cave. It was still too dark to walk along the trail to the tree, so he made a fire and brewed coffee. The warmth of the fire felt good against his hands and face.

"Winter will be here soon. We need something better than a lean-to if we want to survive the snows."

After two cups of coffee, it was light enough to walk. He put everything back in the pack, laid the pack on the ground with the shoulder straps up, sat down and leaned back on the pack while putting his arms through the straps. He cinched the straps tight against his chest, rolled over on his stomach, and then crawled over to the cave wall. He used the incline of the wall to help him stand.

"I could sure use my walking stick right about now."

Bending over to balance the pack on his back, he walked along the trail. At the tree, Blades picked several of the fruit, and leaned against the tree as the sun broke over the horizon. The warm rays felt good against his face as he watched the water flowing west towards the horizon. He saw a small sumac tree leaning out over the river.

Blades took off the pack and cut down the tree using his pocketknife. He stripped the shaft of its branches, and cut the smaller end to the right length for a walking stick.

"Perfect. I think I have a new profession. Royal walking stick maker!"

Putting the pack on was much easier with the aid of the walking stick. The stick made walking easier, but he still needed to walk at a slow pace to keep his back from hurting. It was nightfall when he arrived at the beach.

Eating berries along the way had given him strength and he was not hungry as he sat down on the sandy beach. He spread out two of the blankets, layed down, and then used two blankets to cover himself. The night air was cold and he pulled another blanket over his face to keep warm.

"Ty, wherever you are, I hope you are warm."

CHAPTER 23

Day 15

Blades awoke cold and shivering as the dew settled on everything around him. He built a fire and warmed his hands and feet before brewing coffee. When he saw the shell of the turtle he had eaten four days earlier, he realized he was hungry. Fishing out the last packet of peanuts, he crunched the nuts between his teeth, savoring every crunch until a smooth crème was left.

After drinking the coffee, Blades put on the pack and set out for the waterfall, stopping often to rest.

"I wonder if Ty will be at the waterfall? What if he's not there and I never see him again?"

He thought about how, after the left the site of the house, when Ty dove under the water he wondered if he would ever see Ty again.

It was nightfall when Blades heard falling water pounding the pool below, and hurried to see if Ty was waiting. When he arrived at the camp, a fire was burning, but Ty was not there. Blades scanned the ridge and saw Ty silhouetted against an almost dark sky. A wave of relief washed over him and he shuddered.

Blades liked to think he was self sufficient, but knew he needed Ty and was glad to see him. He was also glad to see a cooked fish lying on a rock next to the fire.

Blades devoured the fish and was looking for

something to drink when he found several cans of sardines and three moon pies. He was still hungry, but the thought of sardines and moon pies together made his stomach churn. He ate two moon pies before he realized he was no longer hungry. As Blades threw the wrappers in the fire, Ty emerged from the shadows.

"Hey, Ty, how did your day go?"

"What do you care?"

Blades was surprised Ty was still angry after being alone for two days. "Look, I was just trying to let you talk. I have bad days too. There are many times when I just want to give up and call it quits."

"What do you know? You've never lost everything, because you don't need anything."

Ty was not in a reasonable mood, but Blades wanted to heal the rift between them.

"I know what it's like to wrestle demons, I wrestle them all the time."

"The demons you wrestle with are yours and yours alone. I can't take them from you. I don't want to take them from you. Maybe you need to talk to God."

The words sliced deep, and then spread salt in the wound. Blades felt his face turning red and his ears becoming hot as the combination of pain, worry and anger boiled to the surface.

"God!" Blades erupted. "And just what God would that be? Your God? The one that looks down his nose at everybody. The God that creates you to fail! Your God is a losing proposition. No matter which way I go, your God screws me. If this God of yours exists and I anger him, I'm screwed. And if this God of yours doesn't exist, if there is no God, I'm screwed. No matter which way I go I'm screwed."

As Blades, spoke emotions swelled and adrenaline coursed through his body. The volume of his voice rose and his hands started to tremble as anger welled in his eyes.

Blades stood and turned from the fire. As he walked out of the circle of light, he stumbled on a small rock, but recovered before his hand reached the ground. Pain shot from his back down his left leg, but his anger squashed it as fast as it had surfaced, and he continued to walk into the darkness.

Religion can conjure the best of demons and Ty had conjured the strongest of all; the God demon. The demon that casts the role of Supreme Being as spoiler; tyrannical ruler of all, with regard for none. Only this demon could torture a man's soul with such ferocity, and Blades knew the demon well.

When he was far enough from the fire to disappear into the night, Blades turned and walked down the path to the river. He felt hurt, angry and confused.

What just happened?

The moon was low in the sky and cast it's reflection across the small waves moving down river. Blades eyes were still too blurred by tears of anger to take in the magnificence of the setting.

He reached over to find a small rock to skip across the water, and as his fingers penetrated the grass, the earth beneath him gave way, plunging him headfirst into the water. Blades was stunned by the water's cold embrace, and he gasped, sucking a cold gulp of water into his lungs. Choking and coughing caused him to inhale even more water, the second rush of water numbing his warm lungs.

The disorientation caused by the cold water cleared, and Blades realized he was in water. The current was strong and it was impossible to figure which way was up to the surface. He remembered his pilot training for ditching, "Exhale and follow the bubbles to the surface."

Blades opened his mouth and exhaled, but only water came out. It was too dark to see any bubbles.

So this is the end. How ironic. I always thought I would die in an airplane, not a river. This is not like what I thought it would be. No pictures. No white light. No fear. It is all so calm.

Adrenaline revived Blades and he screamed, but there was no sound and no one to hear. A presence surrounded him, wrapping him in a blanket of calm, and he settled into a deep, dreamless sleep, the pulse in his ears fading to nothing.

And Blades could breathe no more.

CHAPTER 24

Ty was stunned as he watched Blades walk out of the light and fade into the darkness.

"What the hell was that all about?"

Ty peered into the darkness but could not see, or hear movement. He picked up a stick and stirred the coals of the fire.

"What is he so touchy about? All I said was he had to solve his own problems. I can't spend all my time babysitting him. I have my own problems."

Ty stood and shook his fist at the night stars. "God damn you! Why can't you cut me some slack! Why can't you just leave me alone for a while? I don't need you always testing me, taunting me. Cut me some God damned slack!"

The anger in the caldron called Ty, boiled until it overflowed. Ty shook his fist at the night sky and screamed, "God damn you! God damn you! God damn you to hell!"

The anger continued to boil and Ty looked around for something to hit. He picked up the stick and hit the lean-to, causing it to collapse, scattering leaves and branches. He beat the lean-to as it lay on the ground, and then turned and started hitting the logs in the fire. Sparks flew in all directions, some rising with the smoke into the sky, making little stars of their own. Ty continued to beat the fire until a few embers were left, the fire's warmth extinguished. Seeing the lean-to lying on the ground fueled his anger, causing him to stomp the ground. Over time, Ty's rage diminished and he started feeling guilty for cursing at God. He was still angry, but his guilt turned to despair as he lay down on what was left of the lean-to.

"What will I do now? I do not want to be alone. I want my family. I want it to be the way it was. I want this all to go away."

Ty drifted off to sleep, too tired and too confused to worry about what would come. He wished that nothing would ever come again, but he feared death and what punishment might wait for him.

CHAPTER 25

Day 14

Ty did not sleep well, and awoke before dawn to find himself alone. Blades' bed was empty and had not been disturbed. Ty suppressed the guilt and fear that started to rise by ignoring them.

"Boy, I must have really ticked him off. Well, he's a big boy and can take care of himself. When he gets back we'll straighten everything out."

But, the combination of guilt and fear were still there, lurking under the surface like a ravenous school of piranha waiting to feed on anything that stuck as much as a finger below the surface. The lethal duo was always there; inviting Ty to take a risk, and then amputating a piece of him when he ventured into new waters. Ty hated them, and had cursed the God responsible for their creation. Despite his pious ways and church attendance, Ty had cursed the God responsible for human suffering all his life, and now it was out in the open for all to see. His devotion to God turned into anger, and the anger into hatred.

"I hate you! I hate all that you have made! God damn you to hell!"

Ty spent the day going back to the plane and getting more food and blankets. His arm had healed enough that he could carry the backpack without pain. Staying busy kept the dual demons at bay, but he dreaded the coming night when he knew they would broach the surface with luminescent eyes, like that of a crocodile. He knew he could not turn his back on them, or they would jump out and devour him. He no longer feared life; he was consumed by his sentence to hell.

Ty returned to the camp just as the shield of day disappeared over the western horizon. The camp was as he had left it, with the lean-to still in pieces on the ground.

The cold shroud of night descended as Ty rebuilt the fire. Each time he placed another log on the fire he thought of Blades, and wished he would return.

"What if something happened to him? Don't be stupid! Blades can get through anything."

Concerns for Blades continued to cross Ty's thoughts, but each time he managed to dismiss them and think about something else.

As night closed in tighter, Ty's anxiety started to grow and he thought about all the times he and Blades had faced danger together. About all the times when they relied on each other to get out of a tight situation. Blades had been angry in the past, but always cooled off and let things be forgotten. It was not the first time Ty had seen Blades erupt, but it was the first time Blades had stayed away for such a long time. As night started to press on his flesh, Ty's fear grew. He could not hold back the tears as he looked at Blades empty bed; and the blankets he had folded to make amends. Waves of regret washed over him.

"How could I have been so cruel? How could I have hurt him so deeply?"

Ty blamed himself, because to think the alternative was too frightening. Sleep eluded him, and he awoke every fifteen minutes to see if Blades had returned. Each time the bed was empty and his sorrow

128

grew.

"Wherever you are, Blades, I hope you are warm."

CHAPTER 26

Day 13

The night was long, but at last, daylight washed the stars from the sky. Ty emerged from his refuge of blankets to look for Blades. He followed the stream to the river and then walked down river for two hours before returning to where he started.

The ground of the path was hard, and Ty did not see footprints or signs of human passing. As he walked upriver along the bank, Ty saw where a portion of the bank had caved into the river. In the exposed mud were claw marks where something had tried to climb up the slick bank. The picture of Blades trying to claw his way out of the river, and then being washed downstream, flashed through Ty's mind. He feared his worst nightmare had come true, and that he was alone.

Ty examined the grooves in the mud again, and then sat down in the grass, tears welling in his eyes. He was a grown man, sitting on the bank of a river crying, and he didn't care. He regretted all that he had said, and all that he hadn't said. He regretted opportunities lost. He shed tears for Blades, for himself, for all the lonely nights ahead, and all the moments of beauty he would not share. The frightened cry of a child is painful to hear, but the adult cry of regret contains pain far beyond that comprehendible to a child.

Ty regained his composure and started walking down river to see if he could find Blades' body. After three days, he returned to the camp at the base of the waterfall. As he walked on the trail that led to the waterfall, his hopes rose that he would find Blades sitting beside the fire. When he arrived at the camp, the fire was cold and the camp was empty.

Enough time had passed that Ty had become numb to the pain of loneliness. The pain had not lessened, but he had come to accept it as part of his being.

As the day ended, Ty climbed to the crest of the ridge and looked at the end of day. He was alone, with no one to talk to. It was not by choice, but by circumstance, that he was alone. He wished it were different, but his wishes had little effect on the ebb and flow of what was.

As heavy a burden as loneliness was, it was not the crushing burden of controlling destinies. When he pondered his fate, he looked into the eyes of the controller of destiny and saw true loneliness. Absolute power was absolute loneliness and he regretted cursing the only one who knew he existed.

In his loneliness, Ty knew he was a child of the keeper, a descendent of the breath. When he was alone he felt that breath on his face, heard it in his ears, and breathed it in his chest. And he was afraid. Afraid of what he was. Afraid of what he had been. Afraid of what he would become.

Ty went back to the camp and lay in his bed amongst the pieces of what once had been, and started the next phase of his life. In a moment, things had changed. When he thought it couldn't get any worse, it did. He was glad thirty days ago he didn't know what the future would bring. He was glad that he didn't know what the future would bring in thirty more days. But the bed felt good and he drifted off to sleep without a care. He didn't care anymore and slept as he had when he was a child. There were no dreams.

"Wherever you are, I hope you are warm."

CHAPTER 27

Day 10

Ty became acclimated to his new way of life. At times, he longed for companionship, but also found there were many aspects of himself he had not discovered. He took time to listen to the voice within himself that for so long had been silenced. The voice was wise and compassionate and explained many of the mysteries that had escaped him. He came to know himself and to respect his capabilities and talents. He came to peace with himself. He came to be.

He resurrected the lean-to and built sides on it to form a crude cabin. Every evening Ty climbed to the top of the ridge and watched the day depart as the moon rose, amazed at how his measure of time had disappeared. He no longer thought in days of the week, or weeks of the year, but in day or night, new moon or full moon. Day flowed from night, and night from day, without interruption, and Ty sensed the tidal flow of being. His lack of a perception of time seemed more natural, and he no longer thought of past or future, but of the present. Tomorrow may or may not come, and yesterday was already gone. He no longer experienced urgency, but learned to savor the moment, and found it incredible that he had spent so much of his life worrying about time. Time was an illusion created to measure productivity, progress, or to estimate the amount of life left. The concept of time had become meaningless and life wasting. There was no time. There was life and loss of life. Life spent concerned about time was life lost. Life spent mourning the loss of time was life lost. He felt it ironic that he had spent a great part of his life concerned with something that did not exist. He remembered limiting his sleep at night so he had more time during the day. Now he slept until he awoke and was able to enjoy and participate in every moment of his life. He moved through time without effort and could not imagine what demon had possessed him to worship the time god.

Ty walked back to the cabin and stoked the fire. As he looked at the moon overhead, he saw movement out of the corner of his eye. A figure, squatting across the fire, stirred the coals with a stick. Ty froze, not knowing if the figure was real or imaginary.

"Oh, I'm real enough," the figure said in a man's voice.

Ty froze and watched the figure, wondering if the solitude had driven him insane.

"No, you have not lost your mind," the man said.

The figure was too small to be Blades. His head was covered with a hood, with only the tip of his nose, and right hand visible. The fingers were long and slender, yet strong.

"Who are you?" Ty asked.

The man did not answer as he continued to stir the coals.

"Who are you? What is your name?"

"You may call me what you will. What would you like to call me?"

The answer irritated Ty; he did not like games.

"Are you God?"

The figure chuckled. "No, I am not what you call God."

Ty was relieved, but confused. "What do others call you?"

"Most call me Shaman."

"Where did you come from?"

The man looked up from the fire. "I've been watching you.

Ty could see the man's face was brown, as if weathered by the sun, and he had brilliant green eyes. His lips were thicker than Ty's, and he did not have any facial hair.

"Watching me? How long have you been watching me?"

"Long enough."

"What do you mean long enough? How long?"

The figure did not answer.

"How long! Hours, days?"

"All your life."

Fear started to rise in Ty as he looked at the figure squatted before him. "What do you mean, all my life? We've never met before, how could you know me all my life?"

"We have met a thousand times, but you do not recognize me."

Ty tried to recall ever seeing the man's face. As he thought, he recognized something familiar in the man's voice.

Shaman raised the tip of the stick in the air. "Ahh! You are starting to remember."

"There is something about you that seems familiar."

"It is not my face that you will recognize."

"It seems as if you know what I'm thinking, Mr. Shaman."

Shaman smiled and went back to stirring the fire. "Do you not recognize my voice?"

"Yes, in a way. It seems so familiar, and yet so strange."

"Strange, or distant?"

Ty moved closer. "I have a thousand questions to ask you."

Shaman raised his hand, signaling Ty to stop.

"Is something wrong?"

"You must first remember me, before we can go further."

Ty flared his eyes and turned his hands palm side up in frustration. "How can I remember you? I told you, we have never met."

Shaman pulled the stick from the fire and pointed at Ty with the glowing tip. "You must remember. We have talked many times."

Ty cocked his head to the side and gestured with his hand. "On the phone? In person? How many times have we talked?"

"Many times. We will talk more when you remember."

Ty lowered his hand and let out a long breath.

Shaman rose and walked toward the waterfall.

"But I have so many questions to ask you!" Ty shouted as Shaman disappeared into the dark.

"When you remember. Then we will talk again."

Ty sat in stunned silence. Again, in a moment, life had changed. He was alone, but no longer alone.

Ty lay on his bed, looking at the fire through the openings between the branches in the front wall. The flames danced in the cool night air as he drifted off to sleep.

In sleep, Ty recognized Shaman's voice, and bolted upright. It was Shaman's voice that he heard between waking and sleeping.

"Shaman! I remember! I remember who you are!"

Ty raced outside but Shaman did not reappear. Ty waited beside the fire until the first light of dawn, then went in and slept, dreaming of his family, Blades, and Shaman.

CHAPTER 28

Day 9

Ty awoke hungry and found the fire cold. He built a new fire, then caught and cooked four trout, saving two for Shaman. Unlike days passed, Ty awaited nightfall with anticipation at the expected reappearance of Shaman. He was once again filled with hope.

The sun seemed unwilling to release the realm of earth to night, and the hours passed in slow dirge. Ty walked back and forth from the camp to the river, just to pass the time. As sure as water returns to the sea, night follows day. The sun's grip loosened and night flowed into the camp. Ty became nervous as he waited for Shaman to appear. At the emergence of the first stars, Shaman walked into the circle of light cast by the fire.

"I remember! I remember!" Ty shouted.

Shaman walked toward Ty with a smile. "I knew you would."

"I have so many things to ask you. But first, are you hungry?"

"No, but thank you for asking."

Ty gestured to the fish lying beside the fire. "I have some fish if you are."

"No, thank you very much," Shaman said as he sat down next to the fire, "I am not hungry."

Ty sat in the same spot as the previous night, not too close, but not too far from Shaman. "I have so many questions, but the first one I want to ask is, am I dead?"

"Do you feel dead?"

"No, but I don't feel the same as I used to feel. I'm in the shadow world, aren't I?"

Shaman gestured at the shadows on the trees created by the fire. "Yes, there are shadows made by the fire."

"No, I mean I'm not in the world of the living."

"Do you not feel alive?"

"Yes, I feel alive."

"Then you are in the world of the living."

"But I'm not with my family."

"Correct, you are separated from your family."

"And I'm not with Blades."

"Correct, you are separated from Blades."

"Where are they?"

"They are not here."

"I know they are not here, but where are they?"

"They are not here," Shaman said again.

"Are they alive?"

"Of course,"

"But they are not alive here?"

"Do you see them?"

"No."

"Then they are not alive here, are they? Your

perception of life is too small."

"Will I see them again?"

"Your perception of life is too small," Shaman answered again. "All things in good time. What other questions do you have?"

"Why am I here? Why are you here?"

"You are here because you are. I have come to guide you on a journey."

"A journey?"

"Yes, a journey," Shaman said, then held up his hand with his palm facing Ty, "But not yet. The time is not right."

"Where are we going?"

Shaman did not answer, but instead started stirring the fire again.

"When is the time right?" Ty continued.

"When it is right. It is not yet right."

For the first time, Ty relaxed and leaned back against a small tree. "When will it be right, and where will we go?"

And who will we meet there?

CHAPTER 29

Blades knew that there comes a time in every person's life when they must look into the eyes of death. The moment may come at the realization the end has crept up on them, or it may come the split second before breath departs. The time had come for Blades.

Fear, remorse, anger, and desperation attacked and overwhelmed Blades. He had faced death many times in the past, but this time it was different; this time he felt death's grip on his arm and for the first time knew his own mortality. For the first time in his life, Blades was alone.

To die held no power over Blades, but to die alone terrified him. It was an irrational fear for when death arrives everyone is always alone. For Blades, it was important to be missed, important to be mourned, important to be loved. For all his life, Blades had searched for that one thing that would give him meaning and purpose. Now, alone in the darkness, he discovered it was love, and he ached at the irony. To discover he needed love, when he was alone, was the cruelest of ironies.

Blades lashed out and screamed a shrill cry. Not even the dead missed the cry, and they knew it too well. They had heard the cry of torment many times before when a soul realized its failure at life. The cry pierced the common soul of all men, and the pain of one became the pain of many.

Blades did not realize how great the pain might

have been, if others had not wicked much of it away from him. What he felt was the pain of his entire life concentrated into one moment.

The pain overwhelmed Blades, and he reeled like a fighter stunned by the well-placed punch of an opponent. However, the opponent had an unfair advantage; it possessed the weapons of wisdom, strength, and overwhelming size. Blades was an infantile opponent, and in his moment of defeat, he recognized his error. He opened his mouth to cry for help, but nothing came out.

CHAPTER 30

Shaman continued to stir the fire. "The time will be right when the time is right,"

"Why do you need to lead me anywhere?" Ty asked as he moved closer to the fire.

Shaman did not answer.

"You like playing with the fire, don't you?"

Shaman tilted his head and Ty could see the corners of his mouth turn up into a smile.

"Yes… yes I do," Shaman said before looking back into the glow of the coals.

The thought that Shaman could be evil entered Ty's thoughts, but before he could speak, Shaman spoke.

"No, I am not evil."

"How do you do that? How do you know what I'm thinking?"

"It is not hard."

The answer raised more questions in Ty's thoughts, but he decided not to ask them for the time being.

"You're not from here, are you?"

"I'm sitting here, aren't I?" Shaman answered.

"Yes, you are, but you come here from somewhere far away, don't you?"

"What do you mean far away?"

"I mean, you're not like me, are you."

In some ways we are the same, and in some ways we are different," Shaman said as he rocked his head from side to side.

"You're not human."

"No, I'm not human," Shaman answered.

"Do you have fire where you come from?"

"No, I do not."

"So, playing with fire is one of the enjoyments you get when you come here."

"Something like that."

"Who are you and where do you come from?"

"All is not as it seems," Shaman answered as he looked up from the fire.

Ty could see kindness in Shaman's face and moved closer, waiting for Shaman to signal him to stop, but the signal never came.

"What do you mean by that?"

"You view life from your perspective, but your perspective is flawed."

"It is the only perspective I have."

"Yes, but it is a limited perspective. Your perspective is the sum of your experiences and teachings."

"But that is all I know."

"Exactly. You misperceived what actually occurred on many occasions, leading to a misperception of what is. What is real is clouded by what you perceive to be real."

"How do you know this?"

"Life continually sent you course corrections," Shaman continued. "Many times the corrections were painful. When you failed to learn the lesson, and held on to your misperception, you were destined to repeat the lesson until you learned the truth."

Ty shifted and looked down into the glowing coals so that Shaman would not see the fear welling within him.

"You talk as if my life is past."

"Your life has passed. Your life passes every second of every day. That which was, is no more and will never come again."

"You make it sound like a runaway freight train, headed into oblivion."

"No, it is more like the natural progression of the sun and moon. You view your life in spurts, when it is a continuous flow like water returning to the sea. You can no more hold back the flow of your life than you can the flow of water."

"I have felt this these past days."

Shaman smiled and nodded in acknowledgement.

Ty shifted again and looked into Shamans eyes with a sense of helplessness. "So you are here to lead me?"

"Yes."

"Lead me to a lesson?"

"Yes."

"Will the lesson be very painful?"

"No, quite the contrary. You will find the lesson quite pleasant."

Ty felt relieved. "Why do I need lessons? What is the purpose of all this?"

"You are the purpose of all this."

"What do you mean by that?"

Shaman held up his hand to motion stop, and then stood. "All in good time, all in good time."

"Is this the end of our talk tonight?"

Shaman turned and walked into the darkness.

"But you could stay and play with the fire," Ty called after him.

Shaman turned with a smile across his broad, brown face, and then chuckled before continuing to walk away.

"When will I see you again?"

"When the time is right," Shaman answered from the darkness.

Ty thought about following Shaman, but the darkness seemed to close in around him like walls of a prison. He listened for Shamans footsteps, but heard only the wind in the trees. Darkness seemed to close in tighter and Ty retreated to his cabin where he lay down and watched the fire. A sudden wind swept down and blew the fire out, leaving Ty alone in the dark. He pulled the blankets over his head and escaped into the solitude of sleep.

CHAPTER 31

Day 8

The call of a Cardinal perched on the roof awoke Ty. He looked through the openings in the roof at the bright red feathers and smiled.

"My own personal rooster. How are you little fellow?"

The Cardinal looked at him with one eye, then sharpened its beak on a branch in the roof.

"Are you hungry? I wish I had some birdseed for you — wait! I have an idea."

Ty walked over to the edge of the stream, and used his fingers to dig into the soft dirt. After several handfuls, he pulled a worm from the soil, holding it up for the Cardinal to see.

"Here you go little fellow."

The Cardinal flew from its perch and snatched the worm from his fingers. He watched in amazement as the bird disappeared over the ridge. After several minutes, the Cardinal reappeared, landed on the roof of the cabin, and called out again.

Ty laughed and shook his finger at the bird. "Don't get greedy now."

The bird looked back, then sharpened its beak on the branch again.

"O.K., one more, but that's it. I have to get my own breakfast."

Ty dug up another worm and the Cardinal again

scooped it up and flew into the trees. He waited for the bird to return, but it did not come back.

"Maybe he understood."

He called toward the ridge, "Come back tomorrow, and I'll give you some more."

Ty busied himself to keep his mind occupied until night arrived. He hoped Shaman would return because he wanted to ask him about many things. When light no longer filtered through the trees, and shadows filled the hollow, he climbed to the top of the ridge. As the sun disappeared over the rim of the earth, he marveled how everything flowed together.

"It is beautiful," a voice said.

Startled, Ty turned to find Shaman sitting beside him. "Wha…? How…? How did you get here? What are you doing here? It is not night yet."

"The same thing you are, watching the sun paint the sky. Do you want me to go?"

"No. I just didn't expect you yet."

"I'm here because you called."

"When did I call?"

"When you wished there was someone here to share this with you. You did wish it, didn't you?"

"Yes…yes I did, and I am, glad you are here. How long will you stay?"

"It is time for me to stay with you as long as you desire,"

"I would like for you to stay with me all the time. But I have a question I need answered. How do I know I can believe you?"

"Go ahead, ask it?"

"Ask what?"

"Am I evil?"

Ty was stunned. Shaman knew what he was thinking before the thoughts were formed in his head. "Well, are you?"

Shaman chuckled. "Evil, that's a good one. What you call evil should be called what you don't like. A better distinction of good and evil is truth and untruth. That which moves you closer to your purpose is truth. That which moves you further away from your purpose, or stagnates you, is untruth. I bring you truth."

Ty shifted and looked at Shaman, "Are you saying there is no such thing as evil?"

"Of course not. There is evil all around you. What I am saying is you do not recognize it."

"What do you mean I don't recognize it? I see it every day and recognize it well."

Shaman smiled and put his fingers across his lips, as if to keep something from escaping. The smile irritated Ty. Shaman chuckled and Ty became angrier as he considered how to express his annoyance.

Before Ty could speak, Shaman raised his hand to stop him. "So you think I find myself superior?"

Shaman's statement made Ty furious, "I don't know how you read my thoughts, but it is an invasion of my privacy and I want you to stop!"

Shaman smiled, lowered his hand, and looked into Ty's eyes, "How do you expect me to not listen when you shout so loudly?"

"I'm not shouting, I'm thinking, and that is a private matter."

"You want me to stop listening to your thoughts?"

"Right! My thoughts are my thoughts, and secrets for me to know."

Shaman gestured at the fading vestiges of the sunset, "Is this only for you as well?"

Ty shook his head, "Of course not, beauty is for everyone to enjoy."

Shaman touched his brown forehead with a finger, "Just as beauty is not private, neither are your thoughts. It is not within my power to ignore this sunset and it is not within my power to ignore your thoughts. Nothing is private, not even your thoughts. But, we are straying from the subject. We were talking about evil."

Ty felt threatened, "What do you mean nothing is private?"

Shaman raised his hand again, "That is a subject we will discuss later, for now, let us talk about evil."

Ty started to protest, but the look on Shamans face told him the subject would not be discussed further. Ty respected authority, and everything about Shaman conveyed authority. Ty did not feel threatened by Shaman, but knew when Shaman said something would not be discussed, it would not be discussed.

"Evil is everywhere," Ty continued.

"Such as?"

"Well, what about those things that kill us? How can you call those things that cause death, truth or untruth?"

"You don't believe in accidents?"

"Of course there are accidents," Ty responded.

"Automobile accidents kill. Are they evil?"

The question made Ty uncomfortable and he wished he had chosen another topic for their discussion. "No, I guess automobile accidents are not evil."

"Are you sure?"

The uneasy feeling in Ty grew stronger, "Well, some accidents could be considered evil, such as when someone is drunk, or did some other irresponsible act."

"Really?" Shaman responded. "Do you think that man has the capability to develop cars, or other means of transportation, that would not result in as many deaths?"

"Yes, I guess so."

"Then why don't you do it?"

Ty squirmed and felt as if he were being cross examined.

"Probably because it would cost too much."

Shaman put his finger on his chin, "What is too much? What is the value of a human life?"

Ty squirmed even more and felt this was a non-winnable argument, "No value is too much."

Shaman raised his finger and shook it in the air,

"Mankind has the capability to develop a safe means of transportation but does not because it would cost too much. Do you see the evil here? It is not that accidents are evil; it is placing a financial value on life that is evil. Do you suspect the rich place the same value on their lives as they do on the lives of the poor?"

Ty felt the finger was being pointed at someone else and his feeling of indictment lessened.

"No, probably not."

"Do you not see the evil?"

"Yes, but what about disease?" Ty asked.

"Such as what?"

"All the diseases that plague man."

Shaman cocked his head, "You mean such as sexually transmitted diseases."

Ty blushed, "No, I can see where those are the responsibility of those that contract them, but I mean other diseases such as cancer and heart disease."

"And those are not the responsibility of those that contract them, correct?"

Ty felt he was back on the witness stand again, "Well, heart disease may be the responsibility of those that suffer from it, but what about the other diseases?"

"You feed your children milk that is contaminated with antibiotics, growth hormones and pus, and you wonder why they develop illnesses? You genetically change your food so that not even insects will eat it, and you wonder why you suffer. You eat scavengers that were born to dispose of

156

rotting carcasses, and wonder why illness is passed on to you. Why do you do this? Have you never heard you are what you eat?"

Ty felt accused, "We do it to produce more?"

"Produce more what?"

Ty knew the answer Shaman alluded to, but would not say it.

"That is right!" Shaman said. "You think it in your mind but are afraid to say it. Money. You do it to produce more money."

"We can also feed more people."

"Do you? Do you feed the poor?"

Ty started to perspire and wiped his forehead, "Well, yes."

"Then why do people starve to death?"

Ty looked down at his shoes and thought about all he had eaten that day, "I feel ashamed. I'm sorry I brought this up, and I'm sorry I asked if you were evil."

Shaman patted Ty on the shoulder, "You have not offended me. You needed to see the true nature of evil."

Ty looked back up at Shaman, "It is so hard for us. The Devil always tempts us and causes us to do ill."

"The Devil?" Shaman said as he shook his head, a look of disgust on his face. "It is so easy to blame devils instead of accepting the consequences of your own actions."

Ty again felt accused, "If God did not want us

to do evil, why did he create the Devil?"

Shaman let out a long breath, "That which you call God did not create any devils."

"Are you saying the Devil does not exist?"

"Of course the Devil exists, but that which you call God did not create it."

"Well, if God did not create him, who did?"

Shaman put his hand on Ty's shoulder and smiled, "You did."

CHAPTER 32

The call of a Cardinal sounded familiar, yet strange and far away.

Blades coughed, and water shot from his mouth and nose; his chest heaved as his lungs cleared themselves of the unwelcome intruder, seeking the air they craved. Stomach muscles joined the protest, expelling water and food. His body wrenched, until the spasms diminished and he was able to draw a breath. He felt grit between his teeth and spat to clear his mouth. The thought of putting water into his mouth to rinse it out repulsed him.

Blades was in a foot of water, with his head and left arm draped across a log. His head bumped against the log as his body shivered to warm itself. Looking up he saw green grass protruding over the edge of a bank. He rolled over on his back, resting his head and shoulders on the log. The sun warmed his face, and pumped life back into his body.

Blades did not know where he was or how he got there, and didn't care. He cared about getting warm, and knew if he didn't he would not survive.

Rolling on his left side, he paused to look at the bank and the grass two feet above him.

"I can make that."

He rolled over on his stomach and pushed himself up on his hands and knees. The new position caused water in his lungs to shift and he coughed again until his lungs cleared. The coughing triggered his gag reflex, and he started vomiting water again, continuing until he had dry heaves.

"Wonderful!" he said between heaves. "Just what I need to make my day better!"

Blades rocked back on his heels and looked at the bank three feet away. The thought of warmth gave him strength to lunge at the bank with his hands as he pushed off with his knees. Grabbing the grass with both hands, he pulled the upper portion of his body onto the bank. With a second effort, he pulled the rest of his body out of the water.

The air was warm, but as the water evaporated from Blades' clothes, it caused his shivering to worsen. He kicked off his shoes, pulled off his socks, and then removed the rest of his clothing until he lay naked in the soft grass. The midday sun warmed his body, and a smile crossed his face. He broke off grass and held it to his nose. The smell reminded him of warm summer nights and new mown hay. Fresh cut grass had a unique smell that conjured images of good times.

A bellow of laughter escaped, piercing the surrounding silence. More laughter followed, becoming louder and louder until everything around him was filled with the spontaneity of life. Blades was alive, and he was happy.

Late in the afternoon Blades felt strong enough to walk and knew food would increase his strength. He gathered his clothes and hung them on laurel bushes to dry. On the hillside above were blackberry bushes loaded with ripe berries. He climbed the short distance and feasted on the dark purple berries.

Blades had washed up on the outside of a bend

in the river, where the water had created a sandy beach. He saw laurel bushes extending out from the bank downstream, and knew behind the laurels would be an eddy pool with froth. Froth meant bugs, and bugs meant fish. He walked back to his clothes where he pulled a knife from the pocket of his pants. He cut a sycamore shoot an inch in diameter, stripped the branches, and whittled a sharp point with a barb on the small end. The sun felt good on his back as he whittled, and sweat started to trickle down the sides of his chest. He looked down river, his gaze fixed on the bend around which the river disappeared.

"What a difference from this morning."

It had been a long time since Blades had "danced with death." In his military career he knew the dance well. It was a dance he appreciated, and looked forward to. Much like making love, the dance resulted in a release of exhilaration.

At the end of every mission, he would say, "Cheated death one more time," and continued the tradition after every landing in civilian life.

Blades looked at the river as it flowed to the west.

"Cheated death one more time," he whispered.

But this time it didn't feel the same. He hadn't cheated death, and he knew it. She had given him up of her free will; it was her call, not his. His hollow words hung in the air, drifting like smoke, until they dispersed into nothingness.

The realization that death was no longer the enemy left a void. Without an enemy, there was no hunter. Blades defined himself by his enemies, and in a strange dance, they became the closest of friends, giving each other purpose and definition. He mourned the loss of his enemy. His joy turned to sadness as he realized the enemy had vanished, and with it a good friend.

A growl from his stomach pulled Blades back to the moment, and he started walking, his masculinity swaying with each step. He felt a sense of freedom without clothes, as if there was nothing between him and the rest of the world.

"I could get into this nudist thing, as long as no one else is around."

Blades walked down a deer path along the river, savoring his newfound freedom. He was deep in thought when a small shrub he had pushed aside, snapped back hitting his newfound sense of freedom. He walked the rest of the way with the spear in his right hand, and his left hand covering a much-reserved freedom.

Behind the laurel bushes was a large patch of froth, with several carp feeding on insects. The fish were stationary as they swam against the current and he picked one that looked fat and healthy. Blades lined up the point of the spear at a forty-five degree angle to the fish, then jabbed the point through its side. The fish lunged with a powerful stroke, pulling the spear from his hand. He grabbed the spear and with a heave threw the fish up on the bank. The spear had penetrated through the fish, the barb sticking out the other side.

"I'm sorry it has to be this way, but you, my friend, are going to taste very good."

Blades walked back to his clothes, the spear over his shoulder, his freedom swaying in the breeze, and the fish slapping him on the back. When he reached his clothes, he pushed the spear into the sand in two feet of water to keep the fish alive as he prepared a fire.

Putting on his clothes, Blades experienced another type of freedom. Freedom to move about without fear of injuring the more sensitive parts of his body.

He gathered firewood and tall grass from last year's growth, pulled an eyeglass lens from his pocket, and focused the sun's rays on the small pile. Within minutes, there was a fire that was suitable for cooking.

After cleaning the fish, he suspended the spear and fish over the fire. The fish hung in the heat and smoke from the fire, and within minutes changed color. The aroma of cooked fish filled the small hollow, and Blades' mouth started to water as the saliva glands at the base of his tongue tightened. The feeling in his mouth reminded him of pickles, and his saliva glands tightened more.

The fish started to fall off the spear and Blades removed it from above the fire. He pulled a loose piece from the carcass, blew on it and put it in his mouth, where it dissolved on his tongue. It tasted sweet, and he moaned in ecstasy.

"The finest restaurants in Paris never served up anything as delicious."

He put another piece in his mouth, savoring the flavor and texture. Carp would not have been his fish of choice, but now it was the best fish he had ever tasted. He savored the fish until nothing was left but bones.

The sun approached the mountaintops and night was a few hours away.

"Time to put your strength to work."

Gathering branches, he made a lean-to big enough to cover him. He gathered tall grass for a bed. As night descended, he sat by the fire and thought about how much had changed in one day. He toasted his lost enemy by throwing the bones of the fish in the river, and then lay down on his bed.

"This had been a good day. No, this has been a great day! Ty, wherever you are, I hope you are warm."

Blades drifted into a deep sleep and saw children playing on the other side of the river.

CHAPTER 33

"I did?" Ty shouted. "I created evil? I can't create anything. Why are you blaming me?"

"To whom should I give the credit?"

"I don't know, but don't blame me!"

Shaman smiled, "Why not?"

Ty felt Shaman's smile condescending, and it infuriated him. "Because I didn't do it, and you know it! God created the Devil!"

"Are you sure?"

Ty jumped to his feet. "God damn you! You hypocritical bastard! God damn you to hell!"

Shaman raised his hand. "That is a power you do not have. It is almost dark and we need to return to the camp while you can still see."

"To hell with you, I'm not going anywhere!"

"As you wish," Shaman said as he turned and walked down the path to the camp.

Ty was too angry to sit, so he walked in circles as the horizon faded to black. After an hour, he walked down the path to camp. The night was dark and Ty wandered off the path several times. When he emerged into the light of the fire, he was forty feet from where the path came back to the camp. Shaman sat stirring the coals of the fire.

"Why are you so fascinated with fire?"

"I am fascinated with sunlight," Shaman said. "Everything around us started in the center of the sun, and with fire we allow some of it to return."

"What are you talking about?"

"All of this started as energy in the sun. The sun sends energy and trees store it in the form of wood. Fire releases the energy to return to space, where it originated."

The answer surprised Ty. He realized Shaman was knowledgeable of physics on the subatomic level. He studied Shaman's weathered face and hands.

"Who am I?" Shaman said.

Ty felt embarrassed again. "I forgot you can read my mind, but since you already know the question, yes, who are you?"

"I am Shaman."

"Yes, I know you are Shaman, but where did you come from?"

"The same place as you."

"What place is that?"

Shaman did not respond and Ty knew he was not going to respond. He reached out and touched the arm of Shaman's cloak.

"Why did you accuse me like that?"

Shaman smiled again, "I did not accuse you. If I were your accuser, that would make me your devil."

Ty drew in a breath to calm himself, "But you said I created the Devil."

"Yes."

"But I didn't create the Devil."

"Are you sure?"

"Yes I'm sure."

"I told you, that which you call God did not create the devil, and I do not lie. So who do you think made the creation?"

Ty felt the uneasy feeling again in the pit of his stomach, "I don't know."

"Then how do you know it was not you?"

Shamans question confused Ty. "What do you mean?"

Shaman looked into Ty's eyes, "I mean, who does evil? Does that which you call God do evil?"

Ty looked away to avoid Shaman's penetrating gaze. "No, of course not."

"Then who does?"

"The Devil?"

Shaman laid the stick down, "Quit blaming devils. Who does evil?"

"Man?"

"Correct. So, if man does evil, and not that which you call God, then who do you think created the devil?"

"But we cannot create," Ty protested.

"You create every minute of every day. Without you there would be no creation."

"But that would make us Gods, and we are not Gods."

"Correct, but you are creators."

Ty felt his frustration grow as Shaman's words struck a chord within him, even though they were contradictory to everything he believed.

"God created the earth, not men."

"Correct, but man continued the creation. Were you not taught you have power over the earth?"

"Yes."

"Well, it is true. You do have power over the earth. It is your creation that sustains the earth. You create that which did not exist a second ago, and it is your creation that has brought you to where we are at this moment."

Once again, Ty felt anger and shook his finger at Shaman. "It is an insult to God to claim to be creators."

"No!" Shaman said as he shook his finger back at Ty. "It is an insult to that which you call God to deny the gift that has been given to you!"

Shaman's words stunned Ty and stirred something deep inside. Ty put his head in his hands and tried to speak, but words would not form.

"You do not need to speak," Shaman said. "I understand."

After several moments, Ty was able to collect his thoughts.

"Why would we want to create the Devil?"

"Not the Devil, but a devil. Because you needed someone to blame."

"Why would we need to blame someone?"

"Because you needed to stay blameless."

Ty was once again puzzled. "Why would we need that?"

"Because you want to be gods."

Ty's eyes widened and his vocal cords strained, "What do you mean we want to be Gods?"

Shaman smiled and then laughed, "I meant what I said. You want to be gods."

As the reverberation of Shaman's indictment faded, Ty felt accused, but not angry. He focused his attention on Shaman's face.

"No, that is not an accusation," Shaman said.

"Stop that! I told you to quit reading my thoughts!"

Shaman smiled again and then chuckled, "I'm not reading your thoughts. I am listening to your voice."

"How can you be listening to my voice, when I have not said anything?"

"You mean because your mouth has not formed the words yet?"

"Exactly!"

"Do you hear my words?" Shaman asked.

"Of course I hear your words. What kind of question is that?"

"Do you see my mouth move?"

Ty recoiled in terror and jumped up, as he realized he could hear Shaman's words, but Shaman's mouth did not move.

"How – how did you do that? Are you a ventriloquist?"

Shaman started to chuckle, then opened his mouth to laugh as he slapped his thigh.

"What's so funny? What are you laughing at?"

"I'm laughing at you. Am I a ventriloquist?" Shaman slapped his thigh again. "That is a good one. One that I did not expect. Sit down and I will explain."

Ty sat down and Shaman patted him on the knee.

"It is time you understand who I am."

CHAPTER 34

Ty felt at ease and relaxed his battle taught muscles. He had not realized how tense he was, and relaxing felt good.

"I'm one of the others," Shaman started. "I'm one of the three that guided and protected you."

Ty felt fear as he heard Shaman's words but saw that Shaman's mouth did not move.

"You have nothing to fear from me. Quite the opposite."

Shaman leaned forward and rested his forearms on his knees, "We do not need to speak to talk to each other. I can hear your words before they are formed, as you can hear mine."

"But I saw you lips move before," Ty replied.

"Yes you did, even though I did not move them."

"But I saw them! I saw them move when you spoke!"

"Yes you did, and this is one of your first lessons. Everything is not as you perceive it to be. You saw my lips move, even though I did not move them, because you could not perceive I could speak without moving my lips. Do you understand?"

Ty shook his head from side to side.

"That is O.K., you will."

Ty scratched his left temple, "You said you

were one of the others."

"Yes, I am."

"How many others are there?"

"More than you can comprehend."

The answered raised more questions than it answered. "You said there were three."

"Yes, there are three of us."

"Where are the other two?"

"You will meet them in good time."

Ty decided to speak with thoughts, "When will the time be right?"

"Very good!" Shaman said. "See how it works – see how easy it is."

Ty smiled and nodded.

"It is not time yet. You will meet them when the time is right."

"You keep talking about time being right. Are we predestined? Is that what you mean about being right?"

"No, the time will be right when it is most advantageous to help you accomplish your purpose."

"My purpose?"

"Yes, your purpose. You did not think you, and all this around you was an accident, did you?"

Shaman's words raised a question Ty had thought about many times; is man an accident or is there a master plan. Before he could speak, Shaman answered.

"Yes, I know you have wondered this. Who do you think whispered the question to you as you went to and from sleep?"

"You?"

Shaman smiled a broad smile, but said nothing.

"You were with me in my life?"

"Yes."

"Which parts?"

"All of it."

Ty felt like a child caught with his hand in the cookie jar. "All of it?

"Yes, all of it. There was never a time when we were not with you."

Ty felt angry because his privacy had been violated.

"What do you fear?" Shaman asked.

"Who said I fear anything?"

"You are angry, are you not?"

"Yes, a little."

"If you are angry it is because you fear something. What do you fear?"

Ty knew Shaman's question was valid. He did fear something, but his emotions were too mixed to sort them out.

"I'm angry because I fear I have no privacy."

"Why would you fear that?"

Ty shifted as the uncomfortable feeling

formed in the pit of his stomach again. "Everyone needs privacy. We need time to be alone without anyone watching."

"Alone to do what?"

Shaman's question struck at the cord of Ty's fears and his anger swelled. "Time to be alone! Time to be ourselves!"

The words escaped before Ty could quell them, and he wished he could recall them.

Shaman continued to look at Ty, waiting for more to come.

"Stop that! Stop looking at me like that! It's like you can see right through me!"

Once again, Ty wished he could put the words back in his mouth, and once again, Shaman said nothing.

Ty shifted on the log underneath him and reached out for a stick to stir the fire. Shaman's stare seemed to burn through his skin and Ty turned to avoid the inspection. As he stirred the fire, Ty could feel Shaman's eyes fixated on him.

"What do you want from me?"

Shaman did not respond, and Ty turned to him and shouted, "What do you want from me?"

Shaman smiled a weak smile, "I do not want anything from you. I do not need anything from you. The question is, what do you want from me?"

"I want you to leave me alone!"

"That is not true. Just a few hours ago you asked me to stay forever."

Ty turned and continued to stir the coals of the fire, "That was before I knew what kind of a pain you were going to be."

Shaman did not respond and Ty continued to stir the fire, determined not to be the first to speak. After several minutes, he glanced out of the corner of his eye to see what Shaman was doing. To his surprise, Shaman was not there. Ty turned and looked around the circle of firelight, but there was no sign of Shaman.

"Shaman? Shaman, are you here?"

Shaman did not answer, but Ty remembered the words he had spoken.

"Because you want to be Gods."

CHAPTER 35

The children hid behind the bushes, but Blades could hear their laughter. At last, he caught a glimpse of one of them as they ran between the laurels. Their eyes peered at him through openings between the branches.

"He can see us," one child whispered as the others giggled.

"Who are you?" Blades called across the water. "It's O.K. I won't hurt you. Who are you?"

The voices quieted, then after several minutes, a young girl stepped out from between the bushes. She stared at him and then waved.

Blades froze as he saw deep into her bright green eyes. He recognized her from many encounters — she was death. A smile came across her face, and the teeth of an adolescent shone through her parted lips. She blew him a kiss, then stepped back into the bushes.

Blades jerked as he awoke, then sat up, hitting his head on the lean-to. He looked across the river, the moonlight reflecting off ripples on the water. The children were gone and he was alone with his thoughts. He realized he had been given the gift of life. Not just a reprieve of death, but the very precious gift of life.

Blades thought about the girl and realized what he thought was death, was also the one who gives life. He could not get the vision of her luminescent green eyes from his mind, as he recognized her presence throughout his life. The one he fought as the enemy was the one that had protected him over the years.

Blades drifted back to sleep and into dream. Again, the girl appeared, but this time she walked across the water until she stood on the grass a few feet from him.

"Who are you?" he asked.

"You know who I am."

"No, I do not," Blades said as he tried to hide his fear.

"I'm what you call angel."

"Angel? Your name is Angel?"

The girl giggled. "You may call me that if you wish."

"If I wish? Is Angel your name or not?"

The girl looked at him and smiled. "I do not have a name. I have no need for a name."

"But you said you were called Angel?"

"No. I said I am what you call angel."

Blades pulled back from the girl.

"You are an angel? Do angels exist?"

The girl giggled again. "Do angels exist? As you imagine them? No?"

The girl bent over and pick up a stone from the ground.

"We exist, but we are not what you expect."

"What do you mean, not what I expect. I don't

expect anything."

"White wings and choirs," the girl replied, and then winked.

Blades blushed.

"Ok, maybe I did have some preconceptions, but I didn't think anything like that existed."

"Really, then why did you ask us to sit next to you in battle?"

"What?" Blades replied in horror. "You — you heard that?"

"Of course we heard that. We heard everything you asked us. We heard everything you didn't ask us."

Thoughts raced through Blades mind as he remembered many of the things he had said. "You heard everything?"

"Everything"

Blades lowered his head and looked at the ground. Tears started to well in his eyes.

"I am ashamed of many of the things I said. I didn't know anyone was listening."

"We were there. We were always there. You saw us every day, but you did not recognize us. You passed us on the street, yet never acknowledged our presence."

Blades raised his head. "What do you mean? I never saw you."

"You saw us, but you did not recognize us. You did not want to recognize us."

Blades felt accused of something he had not done. "I never saw you."

The girls smiled and looked into his eyes. "You not only saw us, you talked to us."

"What! I never talked to you. How could I? I didn't know you existed."

"We talked when you were awake and whispered in your ear when you passed to and from sleep. You failed to hear us because you drowned out our presence with the unimportant emergencies of everyday life. Even when you called on us in times of desperation, you ignored our presence."

Blades raised his hands and pleaded with his face. "Honest, I never knew you were there."

"We are always there. We are there when you call for our help, and we are there when you do not call. Even in your darkest hours, we are there."

Blades lowered his hand and looked back down at the ground. "I'm sorry I didn't know you were there. If I would have known, I would have acted different. I'm sorry."

"There is no reason to feel sorrow. You have not offended us in any way. There is nothing you can do that would cause us to abandon you."

"Nothing?" Blades asked as he raised his head and looked into the girl's eyes.

"Nothing. We hear your prayers and always join in your petitions. We will never leave you."

Blades looked deeper into her eyes and felt love. It was not the tension fraught love of male and female, but the all-encompassing love of mother and child.

"Are we what you expected?" the girl asked.

"No."

"No, we are not, but we most certainly are."

The girl turned and threw the stone across the water. The stone skipped five times before it succumbed to gravity and disappeared under the surface of the water.

Blades was impressed by the girl's words, but also by the fact she could skip a rock five times without effort. "That's a viewpoint I've never considered."

"All is not as it seems. You and your place in life are far different than what you imagine."

"My place? I don't know my place. My life is gone, or at least the life I knew is gone. There are still simple pleasures, but for all practical purposes, I am dead."

"Ahh, death," the girl responded. "Death, as you fear it, does not exist. Whether you believe it or not, you never die."

"What do you mean, I never die! We all die. My parents died. My grandparents died. We all die"

"You never die," the girl replied as she turned and walked into the darkness. "But that is a talk for another time."

"Another time?" Blades called out after her. "What other time? Will I see you again? Hello? Are you there?"

It was a dream long in the making, yet short in

the telling. Blades awoke as the sun broached the eastern horizon. He had a clearer vision of life and purpose. He had to find Ty and tell him about the girl.

CHAPTER 36

Ty felt abandoned as he lay on his bed of straw, watching the fire through the openings in the cabin wall. He regretted driving Shaman away, and tears filled his eyes as he struck the earth with his fist.

"You idiot! You stupid, stupid idiot! You killed Blades and now you've driven away Shaman. You stupid, stupid idiot! You're all alone and it's your own damn fault!"

Ty hit the earth with his fist until his emotions broke through and he sobbed as he mourned the loss of companionship; the companionship of his wife, the companionship of Blades, the companionship of all he had known during life. Feeling of loss and despair tumbled out onto the ground, and he hit the earth even harder.

"You stupid idiot! You always have to be right! You always have to know more than everyone else, even when you don't know what you're talking about! Mister better than everyone else! Well now there is no one else, so who are you going to impress now with your piety and goodness now? Who? Mister want to be God! Who will you reign over now?"

Ty's tears washed the earth, but like all showers, came to a finish. He sat up and wished for Shaman's return.

"Shaman, you said you never left me. Are you there?"

Shaman did not answer and Ty felt like a child

bargaining with an adult.

"Shaman!"

"Yes."

Ty spun around, but could not see Shaman. He jumped out of the cabin, but still could not see Shaman.

"Where are you?"

"I am right here."

"Where? I can't see you."

"Where I have always been, right here."

Ty looked around the circle of light cast by the fire. "I still can't see you. Where are you?"

Shaman's voice was calm and reassuring, "I am where I have always been. You cannot see me, but I'm here."

Ty sat down beside the fire and started to sob again. "I'm sorry. I didn't mean to make you mad. I apologize. Will you please come back. I'm so lonely. Please…please come back."

Ty sobbed a lifetime of suppressed tears. When he thought he could cry no more, more tears fell. He thought about holding his wife once more, and tears fell. He thought about kissing his children, and tears fell. He thought about turning the yoke to the left and watching clouds scoot across the horizon.

"Oh, God, I'm sorry! I am so sorry!"

Sixty years of bravado rolled down Ty's cheeks and drenched his shirt. He atoned for a life of arrogance with profound depth of sorrow, until he collapsed on his bed, unable to pay any more.

CHAPTER 37

Day 7

He woke to a world cloaked in dense fog. The fog condensed on the foliage and rained down in large droplets, splattering as they hit the earth. The white miasma muffled sound, creating an unnatural silence. He remembered fog from his childhood; fog so thick that it was impossible to see more than six feet in any direction. This fog was even denser than that. He looked down and could see the ground at his feet, but little more. The fog was disorienting, but not frightening. He had experienced disorientation every day as a pilot, and found the experience amusing. The world was still out there, even though he could not see it.

Ty chuckled as he put his arms out to his side and started sweeping the area around him, shuffling forward until his foot hit one of the rocks in the fire ring. When he turned to the left to walk around the ring, something grabbed Ty's left elbow. He spun around and jumped backwards, falling to the ground. The smell of damp ashes filled the air as he scrambled to a defensive crouch.

"Who's there? Who are you?"

The eerie fog made the silence even louder. Ty reached down and retrieved a piece of firewood lying on the ground next to his foot, but did not move.

Make one sound and I will crack your skull.

He strained to hear his attacker move, but the sound of his pulse pounding in his ears made it hard to hear anything.

Come on, make a sound.

"Why do you think I am your enemy?" Shaman said.

Ty relaxed his arms and stood upright, "Shaman? Is that you? You scared the daylights out of me!"

"Why?"

"Because I didn't know who you were."

"So you assumed I would hurt you?"

"Well, when you don't know, it's prudent to be prepared."

"Preparing for the worst causes you to miss many of the best experiences."

Ty did not answer, but felt he had been chastised again.

"Can you see me?" Shaman continued.

"No, but I know you're there."

"How do you know I am here? You cannot see me."

"I know you're there."

"How?"

"Because I can hear you…" Ty's voice trailed off as the lesson became clear to him. "I understand. Just because I can't see something does not mean that it is not there."

"And?"

"And just because I couldn't see you, doesn't

mean you weren't there throughout my life."

Shaman stepped out of the fog with a wide smile on his face. "This is going to be fun."

Ty returned the smile. "What's going to be fun?"

Shaman laughed deep within his chest. "This is going to be so much fun. It has been a long time since I have been excited. It feels good."

Shaman's excitement was contagious and Ty felt his own spirits lift. "What's going to be fun? What's this all about?"

"Everything is going to be fun, and it is about everything. Very soon you will understand."

"Understand what?" Ty asked.

"Everything," Shaman answered. "Everything."

CHAPTER 38

Blades felt the exhilaration of anticipation as he walked upriver. The sun felt good on his face and arms. He walked along a deer trail on the north bank of the river, but knew the camp was on the south bank. He wanted to cross in the heat of the day, when cool water would quench warm skin.

The trail took Blades inland, around a small hill that had been cut in half by the river. At the top of the hill was a mulberry tree, and Blades stopped to eat. An internal drive pushed him forward, and his step was quick as energy flowed through his body. The brisk walk developed into a trot; the trot into a run. Blades ran over ridges and through hollows with endless energy. He remembered days as a teenager, when he ran to release uncontrollable energy.

After miles of exhilaration, he crested the top of a ridge. The beauty of the east Tennessee Mountains exploded before him on a canvas more magnificent than any found in an artist's studio. The collision astounded him and he stopped, absorbing all that stood before him. As he turned to the south, and then the west, he saw the mountains stretch over the horizon.

"Wow. It doesn't get any better than this."

The internal drive began to re-exert it's never ending pressure, and he turned to continue on his quest.

Two hours before sunset, as he was walking

along the river's edge, Blades saw a meadow on the other side of the river. In the meadow was a small cabin. He froze as he studied the cabin, not sure if it was real or a conjure of his imagination. The drive to move on was replaced with the excitement of possibility.

Blades dove into the river and swam towards the meadow. As he neared the river's edge, his arms and knees hit the bottom. He was so absorbed that he forgot to stand and crawled on his hands and knees until he was on the grass.

The cabin sat in the middle of the meadow, fifty yards from the river's edge. It was constructed of logs chinked with mud, and had a covered porch that extended across the front. There was a door in the middle, framed by two shuttered windows. On the left end of the cabin was a stone chimney. The porch was overgrown with a green vine that hung down, shading a rocking chair. Two steps led up to the porch.

"Hello in the cabin," Blades shouted. "Is anybody there?"

There was no answer and Blades walked through the tall grass.

"Anybody in there?" he shouted again, but again there was no answer.

It appeared no one had lived in the cabin for quite a while. Blades brushed back the vine hanging from the roof and stepped up onto the wooden porch. The vines converted the porch into a small room, and the wall of the cabin was painted soft green by light passing through translucent leaves.

Blades pushed open the door, revealing a single room. A table with one chair was positioned against the far wall between two more shuttered windows. A fireplace was in the wall to the left, and to the right a ladder led to a loft filled with dry grass. Blades sat down in the chair.

Who built this? Who lived here? How long ago did they leave?

Questions raced through his mind, so many that he could not focus on one. He saw a broom made of grass standing in the corner by the fireplace. He brushed a layer of dust off the table with his forearm.

The light of day was starting to fade, and Blades went back outside and walked to a tree line at the edge of the meadow. He found sticks and twigs to make a fire. He peeled bark from a fallen cedar tree to use as kindling. When his arms were full, he went back to the cabin where he put the sticks and twigs next to the fireplace. A piece of flint lay on the stone hearth.

Blades shredded the bark into a small pile. He struck the flint against a rock, and after a few tries, a wisp of smoke rose from the mound. He blew on the fibers and a glow started to grow. Within minutes, a fire brought the chimney to life once more. There fire felt good against his hands and face, and made him feel at home.

The shadows grew and night filled the meadow. Blades climbed the ladder to the loft and lay on the bed of straw. As he looked at the fire, he noticed a mouse on a rafter looking back at him.

"Well, hello little fellow. Where did you come from? Is this your house? If it is, I thank you for your hospitality. It's a very fine place you have. Maybe in the morning we can have breakfast together and talk."

The mouse did not move, but twitched its nose as it looked at the intruder.

"I wonder if you've ever seen a fire in the fireplace. Does the warm air feel good? I have a friend I want to bring here and we can all live together."

Within minutes, the warm air lulled both mouse and man to sleep. The man dreamt of the mouse and the mouse of the man. Neither was sure if the other was real.

As Blades dreamed of the house and the mouse, the girl returned.

"You have given me much to think about," he said.

"There is much more."

"Such as?"

"Whatever you want to know."

"What is my purpose?"

"Your purpose is to seek truth."

"My purpose is to seek the truth?"

"Yes," she answered, a smile emanating from her eyes.

"But what about what Ty calls God?"

"You are free. For many the choice between your will, and the will of that which you call God, is the ultimate choice. The assumption that your will, and the will of that which you call God, could not be the same is an error. The truth is that many cannot bear the burden of freedom. With freedom comes the responsibility of choice. It is much easier for many to invent a god that sits somewhere and does things to them. An eternal adversary that doles out both pleasure and punishment. Usually less of the former and more of the latter. Nothing could be further from the truth. You have been given the power to create, destroy and create anew. You do it every day with every choice you make. With every action you take, and every action you choose not to take. That which you call God has given you the power to create whatever you choose to create. Yet most will choose to sit and watch a few create. Do not blame that which you call God for your decision. Your ability to choose is the greatest gift of all. A few of you will choose to become, most will choose merely to be."

"I see," Blades said. "Does this thing we call God have a plan for us?"

"You mean are you predestined?"

"Yes, I guess that's what I'm asking."

"No. You are the collection of all that you were from the beginning until now. All that you have learned. All that you have experienced. Yet, you are not predestined. It is true that you are shaped by what life has called you forth to do, for life calls forth that which it needs. You cannot ignore the laws of physics, and you cannot ignore your purpose. A fish should not try to be a man and a man should not try to be a fish. You are predestined to be a human in the process of being. How you accomplish that is up to you."

"But what is God?"

"Your concept of that which you call God is infinitely smaller than what is. You have limited that which you call God to fit your misperceptions. You have attributed human traits to that which you call God when that which you call God is not human. Instead, what many do is to reduce that which you call God to a level that can be controlled with contractual agreement or coercion. You try to put space between you and that which you call God, when no space exists. You even practice hatred of each other, which eventually is hatred of yourselves. Hatred prevents you from becoming what you were created to be. There is evil in the world but that which you call God did not create it. You created it."

Blades studied the girl. Her brilliant green eyes reminded him of new leaves in spring. Her skin was smooth and her features delicate. Her teeth were pure white and her hair caught and reflected the sun in a prism of colors. She was the embodiment of femininity as he looked into her eyes.

"What do you see?" she asked, startling Blades.

"I — I don't know," he stammered. "You have given me a much different perspective from which to view the world and my life."

"Look closer," she replied, " and you will see all you want to see."

Instead of embarrassing or intimidating him, her words put him at ease. He leaned closer and saw the answers to every question he had asked, and ever would ask. He saw past and future. He saw what could be, both good and bad. He saw himself as he was and what he could become. He saw love, compassion and truth. He saw all there was to see. His consciousness dissolved into her eyes.

Blades awoke in the straw bed. A robin had awaked him and he listened as it sang the rest of its song. He climbed down the ladder and walked out onto the porch. Blackberry bushes lined the western edge of the meadow, and he put on his shoes before walking toward the sweet smell. He ate until he was full and then walked down to the river to wash his hands. Signs of fall were in the air and trees were starting to pull sap from their leaves to store below ground. It would not be long before the berries would be gone.

Blades walked back to the cabin, and then around it. Wild strawberries grew at the base of the chimney. Remnants of a garden were behind the cabin, but there was no evidence of what had been grown. A bed of ginseng grew along the back cabin wall. He dug some up and sliced it into small slivers to dry for tea.

Back in the cabin, Blades opened the windows and door, and light streamed in, revealing how much dust had collected. He cut back the vine covering the porch to the roofline, revealing the view of the river with the mountains beyond. He swept out the cabin and gathered more grass for the bed.

A small stream, with trout in it, ran along the eastern edge of the meadow. When night fell, Blades closed the door and shutters, then settled into the chair next to the fire. He had everything he wanted, everything he needed. Everything except companionship.

"I have to find Ty and bring him here. No more sleeping in lean-tos. No more dew covered blankets. We could survive the winter here. Tomorrow, I have to find Ty. Ty, I hope you are warm tonight."

The drive was back. The quest had returned.

Blades bid his furry friend goodnight and drifted off to sleep. Again, he dreamed of the mouse and the mouse dreamed of the man, except this time both knew the other was real. And, as he had hoped, the girl returned.

CHAPTER 39

Shaman chuckled. "Death as you fear it does not exist. If there were one thing that would most change your perspective, it would be the realization that you never die. Just as you put on your clothes, so did you put on the thing you call a body. And, just as your clothes will serve you well if you treat them with care, so will your body. Just as your clothes will wear out, so will your body. When your body can no longer serve and protect you from the elements, you will need to hang it back in the closet and return to from where you came. You have put on your body and you will shed your body, but you, the thing that is clothed by the body, will never cease. If you could believe this, you would treat yourself and those around you better. Much better. Whether you believe it out not, you never die."

"If we never die, then where do we go?" Ty asked.

"You mean are there streets of gold?"

"Yes."

"No" Shaman responded. "There are no streets. There is no need for gold. There is no need at all. There is only joy. No sorrow. No punishment."

"No punishment?"

"No punishment. Punishment is a human concept of how to exert power over another. There is no separation, only unity, love and presence.

The concept of no punishment angered Ty. "If there is no punishment, then why did I live a good life?"

"You led a good life?"

"Of course I did. You mean all those people that did whatever they wanted will not be punished?"

"There is no punishment."

"That's not what the Bible says. The Bible says they're going to hell."

"No it doesn't. You have been taught that."

Ty's face turned red.

Another God damned lie! All the nice things I did and all the people I helped! All for nothing! God damn it! It's not fair!

Shaman laughed again. "Not fair? Because people are not going to be punished it is not fair to you?"

Ty blushed

"So you think all the kind things you did were wasted?"

"No, I was good because I didn't want to go to hell."

"What makes you think you led a good life?" Shaman said.

"Well, I did. I was always nice to people."

"Always?"

"Well, almost always."

"So you almost led a good life?"

"You're twisting my words. I led a good life. I was nice to everyone I met."

"You mean you did not feel guilty."

Ty's face turned deep crimson. "I don't like being criticized by you."

Shaman smiled. "What else would you like to know?"

Ty was glad to let the subject go. "How will we know each other in Heaven?"

"There is no need for names," Shaman said. "Names are for differentiation. The intimate familiarity of everyone makes names unnecessary. There is only us and we know each other intimately. There are no families – only one family. There are no husbands or wives – all are bound together. There are no parents or children – all are loved completely. There are no desires – all is present. There are no regrets – all is understood.

Ty sat and looked at Shaman as the enigma poked the coals of the fire. Light from the fire seemed to shine from within Shaman's eyes, rather than reflect off them.

Who is this man? Where did he come from? Is he a man? How does he know these things?

As Ty asked himself these questions, Shaman looked up, his gaze piercing.

"Have I told you the truth?" Shaman asked.

"I don't know."

"Yes you do. You know I have told you the truth because it rang a chord deep within you."

Ty looked back at Shaman, not knowing how to answer.

"Didn't it." Shaman said.

"Yes. Yes it did."

A noise from up on the ridge captured Ty's attention. He looked up but all he could see was movement of a silhouette against a dark sky.

CHAPTER 40

"I'm glad you are back," Blades said. "I've come to look forward to our talks."

"You are welcome," the girl responded. "What would you like to know?"

"Why is there hatred?"

The girl smiled. "Hatred comes from fear. There are but two human emotions, love and fear. Love brings you, and others, closer to that which you are. Fear prevents you, and others, from becoming that which you are. Fear arises out of the unwanted acceptance of the consequences of your own actions, the lack of trust of that which you call God, or a combination of both. When you learn the consequences of your own actions are lessons to teach you of greater things, you will no longer fear.

When you realize that you, and those around you, will never die then you will realize there is nothing to fear."

"But when we are sad are we fearful?"

"Yes. Grief is a combination of fear and remorse. Fear of what has happened and of what is to come. Remorse over missed opportunities. Opportunities to express love and affection that were laid aside. Fear that the opportunities will never come again."

"But so many people need pleasures around them to make them happy."

"That is greed. Greed is a result of the fear of not being valuable. By collecting possessions, money, power or other things, many hope to demonstrate how valuable they are. If you understood your true value, you would not need things other than what is necessary to survive."

"But it's not me! I don't have the power to change that."

"There is but one power, and that is the power of creation. Power that moves you to create the complete human you may become. Many confuse repression with power. Repression inhibits the power of creation. The power of creation is the expression of truth. Repression is the expression of untruth. If you wish to stop evil, look where you practice repression. There you will find that which holds you back from becoming. There you will find where you try to hold others back from becoming."

CHAPTER 41

"You don't like women very much, do you?"

The question caught Blades off guard. "What? Of course I do. They're OK."

"OK?"

"Well, it's not like that, I'm not one of those guys."

"I am not asking if you are a homosexual, I am asking if you prefer the company of men to women."

Blades felt relieved. "Oh, I'm sorry, I thought you were asking me if... well, never mind. Yeah, women are fine. I like being around them."

"But you prefer the company of men."

Blades stopped and thought about her question. After several seconds he answered. "Yes, I like the company of men more than women."

"Why?"

"Because women are duplicitous. You can't trust them. I don't want to offend you, but you're not a woman."

"No, I am angel. I appear to you as a girl because it is the least threatening to you."

"Oh, I don't know about that. You can be pretty intimidating."

"Back to the question. Why do you not trust women?"

"Because you can't. When I am around men, there is not the tension that is always present around women. I don't have to worry about offending someone or having them think I am flirting."

"Did that happen quite a bit?"

"Not quite a bit, but enough that I learned my lesson."

"Not to trust women?"

"Yes. I mean, look at them. It's like their whole life is one big lie with all the makeup, jewelry and clothes. Give me a break. The only women I trust are my wife, my daughter, my granddaughters and my mother."

"But that is it?"

"Pretty much."

"Maybe you do not trust women because they do not trust you?"

"What??"

"Do you like pretty girls?"

"Well, of course. Who doesn't?"

"What about not so pretty girls?"

"Well, maybe not as much."

"Not as much, or maybe you do not see them at all? Maybe women put on makeup, and dress the way they do, because they are ignored by men if they are not a thing of beauty?"

And you claimed not to be threatening. I would hate to see what you were like in the form of a full-grown woman. "I am beginning to see your point."

The girl smiled and then laughed. "So, maybe it is you that is not to be trusted. Maybe those actions you interpreted as flirtations were just one person talking to another."

"But how can you tell?"

"How can you tell when another man is flirting with you? Has it happened?"

"Not that I know."

"What would you do if it did? Would you then be suspicious of all men?"

"No."

"Then why would you abandon women, because you may have been embarrassed once or twice?"

Damn, you should have been a prosecuting attorney. "I never thought about it like that."

"Maybe it is something deeper, maybe you are afraid."

"Afraid? Afraid of what? I've never been afraid of anything in my life?"

"What about God? What about me?"

Blades recoiled. Her smile and innocent looking face had caused him to forget who she was. He tried to answer "no," but the words stuck in his throat.

"I see," she said.

Again, his throat tightened, but he managed to get the words out. "Does God exist?"

"What do you mean by God?" The girl answered.

"You know. White beard, sits in heaven, watches us even when we don't want to be watched."

"No."

"God does not exist?"

"I did not say that, but there is no God as you described."

"Then what is there?"

"Something that you cannot comprehend. Something that is larger than large."

"Try and explain it to me."

"What is it you really want to know?"

"Where do I come from?" Blades blurted.

"Ahh, that is an honest question. I cannot tell you that, but I can paint a picture for you. Picture a large castle that is bigger than anything that you have ever seen. Its walls are longer than the Great Wall of China and are higher than the orbit of a satellite. Now, picture a small grain of sand in the mortar between the bricks in the walls. That which you call God is the castle. You are the grain of sand."

"That is not the God Ty or I were taught."

"I know, and it is sad."

"How big is God? How will I know if I ever see him?"

"That which you call God is not a he nor a she. As a matter of fact, that which you call God does not exist."

"Then, what is there?"

"Existences emanates from that which you call

God. You cannot understand, because you cannot understand nothingness."

"What do you mean by nothingness?"

"Again, I cannot tell you, but I can offer an analogy. In the study of the micro, man has discovered atomic structure and sub atomic particles. With each discovery, a smaller particle was discovered to exist. If you were to study the macro, you would find the same to be true. With each discovery, a larger truth would be discovered to exist. If the study were carried to the ultimate, you would find nothingness."

"If God does not exist and is nothing, then what is God?"

"That which you call God cannot be expressed as an it or an entity. That which you call God cannot be expressed. That which you call God cannot even be expressed as that which you call God. Does this make sense?"

"No – yes — I think so. I think you're telling me that God cannot be labeled, because the label in and of itself is an entity, and God is larger than any entity. Right?"

"Correct."

"But then, why do we label God? Why do we offer religions and doctrines?"

"Because you want to make sense of your world. Because you want to be gods."

"Not me! I never wanted to be a god. Ty was the one that wanted to be god. He was always worshiping and making bargains with God, not me. I never believed God existed."

"No? Then why do you fear me?"

"Because I know who you are."

"Really? Who am I?"

"You are death."

The girl smiled. "You are almost correct, but only because you do not understand the meaning of life."

"What is the meaning of life?"

"You are questioning about a purpose. I'm speaking of a state. They are expressed by the same words, but are two different subjects."

"OK, then what is the purpose of life?"

"You ask a question about purpose, when you do not even understand what life is."

"OK, then what is life?"

"Something you will learn about in the near future."

"Why can't you tell me now?"

"Because I'm not the one to tell you."

"If not you, then who?"

"Someone you least expect."

CHAPTER 42

Blades awoke before sunrise, built a fire, and made tea from the ginseng. The night before, he had placed a rock in the fire. Before going to bed, he removed the rock from the fire, placed it on the hearth, and laid three fish on it. The fish cooked and dried overnight. He ate one of the fish and placed the other two in his pocket.

At first light Blades started walking east, upriver. He walked until he came to a large hickory tree before sunset. He ate the fish in his pocket, then leaned against the tree, and covered himself with grass straw to try and ward off the night chill. He went to sleep and dreamed of the girl.

In his dream, the girl was warning him, but he could not understand what she was saying.

Blades awoke in the middle of the night, shivering from cold. The moon was full and he walked to warm himself. After several hours, he crested a ridge and stepped into sunlight, the sun's rays warming his skin. He stood on the crest, soaking in the warmth, while he looked at the Smoky Mountains. He saw Clingman's Dome, and thought about hiking with friends to the top of the dome. As he reminisced, he recognized something was out of place, but he could not put a finger on it. He studied the Dome and realized it was further south than it should be.

"I am too far north. I am walking in the wrong direction!"

Blades turned and hurried back downriver. As he walked, he tried to piece the puzzle together in his mind.

The river had to carry me downstream. How did I pass the camp without seeing it? And where was Ty's house? We didn't pass any of this on our walk. How could I be east of the camp? This doesn't make sense. Am I someplace else?

Blades decided to put the confusion aside and concentrated on the path ahead of him.

He came to the cabin just before nightfall where he cooked more fish and ate wild strawberries. As he slept, the mouse crawled off its perch and nestled in the straw next to him, and they both dreamed of the girl.

"Then why am I here?" Blades said.

"You are a human in the process of being. You are here for one purpose – to create a complete human.

"What is a complete human?"

A human is not what you own – for you own nothing. A human is not what you control – for you control nothing. A human is not what you see in your reflection – for your reflection is an image of that which houses a human. A human is not what others think of you – for what others think of you is their perception, not reality. A human is not what you think of you – for what you think of you is a perception, not reality. A human is a complete being.

"OK, if I become a complete human, what will happen to me?"

"Once you are a complete human you will have

the freedom to be whatever you want to be."

"But what will happen to me?"

"You will be," the girl answered.

Blades could see the conversation had become a never-ending loop, and there was a more important question he wanted to ask. "Have I been here before?"

"There are some who have walked this earth many times. Many walk this earth for the first time. Neither is better than the other. They just are."

"But have I been here before?"

The girl smiled a loving smile that put Blades at ease. "You have been here many times before."

"But what about other people?"

"What about them?"

"We are all so different."

"Here is the greatest truth, there is no them – there is only us. When you describe angels, you describe yourself for you are one of us. And so are all around you. In your life, you meet nothing but angels. We are of the same family, and have known each other from before the beginning of time. Don't you recognize me now? Don't you remember me calling you from your sleep?"

"I remember you," Blades said. "I remember fearing what you brought."

"What did I bring?"

"Death."

The girl laughed. "I bring nothing but life."

"But life can be so hard," Blades said as he frowned.

"Because you make it so. You were not created to be beasts of burden. You need to take time to enjoy all that has been given you. Enjoy the food you have been given. Preserve life. Respect the sanctity of all. Realize that your needs are of no greater importance than the needs of others. And no less."

"What is next?"

The girl laid her hand on his. "There is one more thing before I go. Many celebrate the birth of a child many years passed. What you fail to see is the birth of every child is joyous. With the birth of every child, a wondrous possibility that far surpasses your wildest dreams is brought to the world. You celebrate the birth of a child so many years ago, yet fail to see that child in every child. Children are a wonderful gift that must be protected. Please don't let them go hungry. Hungry for food. Hungry for shelter. Hungry for love."

With the last word, the girl disappeared.

Blades awoke at first light and the world seemed a different place. He ate some berries with a cup of tea. The sun was cresting in the east when he set foot on the trail.

Traveling was easy compared to when he and Ty had left the airplane. When he became thirsty, he stopped and drank. When he became hungry, he stopped and ate. He no longer looked upon food and drink as a reward, but as something that was necessary to sustain life. It was in the fulfillment of life that he found reward. It was in being, not doing, that he found a natural rhythm that coursed through him, and everything around him. He had changed from trying to subdue everything around him, to being part of it. He counted upon his surroundings to supply him with nourishment when he was hungry, shade when he was hot and shelter when it rained. He looked upon his surroundings as friend, instead of opponent or foe. The warmth of the summer brought the energy necessary to produce the food he needed. The coolness of winter brought the rest and rain necessary for the ground to replenish, just as he needed sleep to replenish. He found a rhythm in life that was soothing and melodious. The anger that had filled him was gone.

As he walked, Blades thought about his newfound freedom and how much he had changed. Movement on the other side of the river disrupted his thoughts. The girl was standing in a clearing of laurels. She motioned for Blades to come, and he dove into the river without hesitation. He had come to trust her guidance, and felt refreshed as the water cooled his skin.

When Blades was a few yards from the shore the girl turned and stepped behind a bush. When he climbed out of the water, she was not there. He looked behind the bush, then up and down the trail. There were neither footprints, nor any other signs that anyone had been there. While it puzzled him, it did not bother him.

"I know there is a reason you called me over here. I don't know what it is, but I know you have a reason."

Blades continued walking down river and came to a large tree after sunset. He sat and looked at the river as a full moon rose, and decided to continue walking until he became sleepy. The night was warm and the moon lit the path. He found it exhilarating to walk with the creatures of the night. When he came upon a herd of deer in a meadow, they raised their heads to look at him before returning to their grazing. He felt at ease as a creature of the day and as a creature of the night.

His pace at night was more relaxed than during the day. Many things that escaped him in the light of the sun were apparent in the soft glow of the moon. He noticed the smell of blossoms as he walked by. Creatures both large and small seemed to move at a more tranquil pace.

He walked all night without tiring, and as the moon started to descend in the west, the first light of day appeared in the east. The prospects of a new day excited Blades, although he did not know why. Something about the new day caused the energy within him to surge, and he started to run to release the energy.

The path was straight and he ran faster and faster until his legs seemed to move like the wheels of a locomotive. The path undulated up and down as the energy flowed from him. He raced up hill as fast as down.

As he crested a hill, the path below him disappeared, and he found himself twenty-five feet above the water. He plunged into the cool liquid and it swirled around him. Unlike the last time he unexpectedly found himself in water, the water embraced him and lifted him to the surface. His head broke through to the air, water cascading down around him like a fish broaching the surface. Unlike a fish that jumps out of water, into air, and then back into the water, he had jumped out of air into water, and then returned to air. Mirror images of creatures that dwelled on opposite sides of the surface of water.

As his lungs filled with air, the answer to the mystery unfolded before him. Like the forces of the Confederate Army during the Civil War, he had mistaken the Holston River for the French Broad River. The Holston and the French Broad rivers join to form the Tennessee River. He had washed up on the northern shore of the Tennessee, and when he traveled up river had missed the confluence of the two rivers. He had made the same mistake, and had followed the Holston, instead of the French Broad.

Blades swam across the river to the southern shore, knowing that the camp and Ty lay somewhere to his left. He walked up the bank to a deer trail, and started on the next leg of his journey.

He did not know how far he had to go, but suspected it was not far. When he tired in the heat of the day, he stopped to rest under the shade of a tree, and fell asleep.

When Blades awoke, the sun was over the horizon and the moon was a large orange sphere above the mountains. He started to look for something to eat, then realized he was not hungry.

"Why waste time eating when I have places to go?"

Blades walked the pace of a man on a mission.

"I can't wait to tell Ty about the cabin."

Blades came to a ridge with a cliff that rose straight up from the river. He climbed the ridge and wondered how much further it was to camp, stopping at the top to triangulate off the mountains. When he crested the ridge, he heard the sound of a waterfall, and his pulse quickened. He looked and saw Ty sitting next to a fire, but froze when he realized someone was sitting at the fire with him.

CHAPTER 43

"Hello in the camp!" a voice shouted from above. "It's me. I'm back!"

Ty looked up at the ridge and saw Blades' silhouette against the stars. The silhouette disappeared into the steep hillside, and Ty could hear Blades descending through the rhododendron. Blades broke through into the circle of light, and both men hugged each other, afraid to let go. They both realized they could not survive without the other.

"I found a great place for us!" Blades said. "It's on the Holston River and has a garden and everything."

The figure on the other side of the fire caught Blades attention as it moved, and Blades froze as the figure moved toward him.

"B, I have someone I want you to meet," Ty said.

"Now it is time to go," Shaman said.

Ty looked at Shaman in disbelief.

"But Blades just got here. We have to fix him something to eat."

"Now it is time to go," Shaman said again. "We have a great distance to cover and you will have plenty of time to eat along the way if you become hungry."

Blades stepped forward. "I don't know who you are, but I have something to tell my friend and I have walked a long way to get here! And just who are you?"

Something about Shaman bothered Blades. Something familiar, yet not quite. As Shaman stepped closer, Blades saw deep blue eyes that flashed luminescent green. Blades froze as he recognized the eyes of the girl.

Shaman put his hand on Blades shoulder, his touch reassuring. He leaned forward and placed his mouth next to Blades ear.

"I heard your cry when no one else could"

Blades froze. The touch was reassuring but the presence was far too close. The color fled from his face and he felt weak.

Ty grabbed his elbow. "Blades, are you OK? Do you need something to eat?"

Blades looked at Shaman.

"If the man says it's time to go, it's time to go. By the way, who is this guy?"

"It's a long story," Ty said with a smile. "I will tell you on the way."

Ty leaned over to pick up a blanket and Shaman put his hand on his shoulder.

"You won't need that."

"But what if it gets cold?"

"If it gets cold I will give you a coat."

"And where are you going to get this coat?" Blades said. "It doesn't look like you're packing a lot of extra gear!"

"Now is the time to go," Shaman repeated. "If you need anything I will provide it for you."

Shaman turned and started walking, while Blades looked at Ty.

"It looks like we're going for a walk," Ty said

"I guess so," Blades replied.

Ty and Blades followed Shaman to the river. At the water's edge Shaman turned to the east and started walking on a path along the riverbank.

Blades moved closer to Shaman. "How far do we have to go?"

"It is a short journey, but we have a great distance to cover."

"You don't talk much, do you?" Blades said.

Shaman stopped, turned around, and removed his hood. His face had a kind look that was reassuring. It was mature, but not old, and his broad brow was framed with short, brown hair. He looked at them without expression, and then a smile came across his face. The smile caused the corners of his eyes to wrinkle, and deep dimples to form at the corners of his mouth.

"The journey will bring you peace and great pleasure." His grin widened and he chuckled. His chuckle evoked warmth and trust.

Ty felt an adventure outside the realm of their small world was in the near future. The possibility of having a future excited him.

The three traveled at a quick, but not hurried, pace. A bright moon illuminated the path. Ty did not talk as he thought about the future.

The future. What a wondrous concept. Two days ago, the future was supposedly known. Yet, today a new future arises. No one knows the future, not even those who seek to control their own destiny. The end of life has no sting. Life without hope, without future, is the enemy. Death lies in the realm of life without the promise of a future.

Shaman had rescued Ty and Blades from certain death.

Blades moved behind Ty.

"Ty, you should see the cabin I found. It has a porch, a fireplace, and a loft filled with straw. It has everything we need."

"I don't think we need anything anymore, B. I think Shaman is taking us someplace where we will meet others."

"You think so? That would be great!"

I have learned a lot from Shaman since you were gone. By the way, were did you go?"

"I fell in the river and washed downstream."

"I thought you drowned."

"I did," Blades said.

"No, I thought you were dead."

"I was."

Ty stopped and turned to face Blades. "But you are here?"

"I know. I drowned and death gave me my life back."

Shaman stopped as Ty and Blades talked.

"You met death?" Ty said.

"Yes, and she is a girl, or at least that is how it appeared to me."

"A girl?"

"She is the most beautiful girl you have ever met. She looks like she is about twelve or thirteen, and she taught me things too."

Ty smiled. "Like what."

"She taught me that God—."

"God? You believe in God?" Ty exclaimed.

"God is not something you believe in or not, God just is," Blades replied.

"That is the same type of things Shaman has been teaching me! What else did she teach you?"

"That we never die."

"I don't believe it! That's the same thing Shaman told me!"

Shaman interrupted the conversation. "We still have far to go, and everything will be made clear to you."

The moon passed overhead and waned as the sun once again announced its authority over the earth. Even in the darkest hour, the sun was master. When out of sight it pronounced its presence with the moon, or reflection from planets.

As the sun rose, Shaman stopped and looked to the horizon. "It never ceases to awe me."

His words were a simple profession of clarity.

"Are you hungry?" Shaman called out without

turning.

"No, I'm good," said Blades.

"Me too," echoed Ty.

Shaman turned, revealing a huge smile.

"Are you cold?" he asked. Both Ty and Blades returned his smile. Shaman chuckled, but this time it conveyed a sense of excitement. The excitement was contagious and both Ty and Blades felt it. It felt like the emotion started in the earth and passed up through their bodies to their minds. It was as if the laughter of Shaman woke a universal excitement.

"We have a great distance ahead of us."

"How great?" asked Blades.

"Great" replied Shaman, his grin widening in anticipation.

It was clear that the trip was to be anticipated with great expectations.

Ty and Blades were occupied by their own thoughts as the sun passed overhead. Just before sunset, the trio rounded a bend in the path and found themselves at a junction with a small road. Shaman stopped and bent down to pick up a handful of dirt.

"Many have passed this way."

"Many?" asked Ty.

"Look at the width of it," Shaman replied. "Many have passed this way."

The sheer contemplation that there were "many" overwhelmed Ty and Blades. Emotions of joy, relief and confusion battled for their place in each man's mind. Before they could ask any questions,

Shaman started walking again at a brisk pace.

"Are we almost there?" Ty asked.

"Yes, but we still have a great distance to go," Shaman replied without breaking stride. "You will see."

Night fell and the three continued without tiring. The road traversed over mountain ranges and through streams. They continued walking through the night and the following day, stopping at the streams for a cool drink, and to watch the sunrise or set. The drinks were not to quench thirst, but to revel in the purity of the life giving water of the mountain streams.

As the moon rose over the mountains, they crested the top of a mountain ridge to see a valley. In a clearing at the base of the ridge were lights.

Ty pointed at the lights. "A city! Civilization!"

Relief, excitement and exhilaration swept through Blades and he stopped walking.

"Why are you stopping?" Shaman asked.

"Because I am not alone anymore," Blades replied. "I can be with you. I can be with Ty again. And I can be with others again."

"You never were alone," Shaman replied as he put his hand on Blades shoulder. "We have been with you always."

"What do you mean?" Blades said.

"Come," Shaman replied. "It has been a long journey. You have learned most of the meaning of life, but wait until you see what is waiting for you."

There comes a time in every man's life when he must accept what he is and what he is not. When he combines those things about himself that he dislikes with the attributes he is proud of, a complete person is born. As they walked toward the lights, Blades put his arm around Ty and they became one. The two halves of the man fusing into a complete human.

CHAPTER 44

As I walked down the hill, the lights moved to the foot of the trail. When I came closer, I saw that the lights were people surrounded by a glow. A sense of relief and excitement washed over me.

A tall man led the group. As I approached him, I put out my hand to shake his. To my astonishment, my arm glowed like those coming toward me. Before I could comprehend the change in my arm, I was standing in front of the tall man.

"Boy, am I glad to see you. My name is Ty, but my friends call me Blades."

The man pushed my hand aside and threw his arms around me, giving me a bear hug.

"And we are happy to see you. But you have no need of a name here. We know you well."

"How do you know me?"

"You are the Centurion."

Centurion. It was a name I called myself, but never mentioned to anyone else. On many mornings when I was younger, before the sun rose, I found myself in the cockpit of a Cessna T210, a Cessna Centurion.

The Centurion was a deceptive airplane as it sat on the tarmac in front of the hanger. Few onlookers would have suspected that in a short period of time, the airplane would be cruising above the clouds at twenty thousand feet, and over two hundred miles per hour across the ground. The airplane was a magnificent steed, with power, grace and attitude. When I climbed into the seat, I felt privileged to be riding such a magnificent creature. The engine had been modified by a master mechanic that also tuned dragsters, and when it started a cloud of smoke belched from the exhausts as the cylinders fired. Then the engine started its characteristic lope. Thump— thump, thump—thump it bellowed, while I completed the preflight checklist and let the turbocharger warm. When I pushed the throttle forward, the lope smoothed out to a vociferous purr that demanded attention. When the final checklist was complete, I would pull out on the runway and push in the throttle half way. The airplane accelerated rapidly, and a few seconds before she was ready to fly, I pushed the throttle all the way forward, the acceleration pushing me back in my seat. The airplane jumped off the ground, waiting for the wheels to come up so it could slide through the air with the grace of an eagle.

As the airplane climbed, I was required to check in with Knoxville departure, who greeted me with "Good morning, Centurion."

"Centurion." I would smile at hearing the sound in my headset, sometimes even saying it aloud. I liked the idea of being a Centurion; a man looked up to by others. It is a desire shared by all men, and as I climbed through the layers of clouds, I envisioned myself a modern day Centurion out on patrol.

"How – how do you know my name?" I asked.

The tall man smiled, but did not reply.

I looked around for Shaman, but could not see him.

"Where is Shaman?" I asked.

"Who?" the tall man replied.

I was puzzled by his response.

"My friend, Shaman. The one who guided me here." I said.

"We saw no one but you coming down the mountain."

"But he was with me. He guided me from the river, through the forests, to you. He was standing beside me when I met you."

"We saw no one. You were in the presence of one of the guides. We hear of them, but cannot see them. Only you can see your guide."

"You did not see anyone with me?"

"No," the man said as he shook his head.

Others gathered around me and shook my hand, or gave me a hug. I was shaking the hand of a small man with a wide smile, when I felt a hand on my elbow.

"Centurion, there is someone who has been waiting to see you," I heard a woman say.

I turned to see a woman who was striking in appearance with fine features, white skin, auburn wavy hair, and luminescent green eyes. Her eyes captivated and held my attention. Her eyes held the same look as the girl's, and her smile the warmth of Shaman's.

"Shaman?" I asked.

The woman chucked.

"Come this way," she said.

"What? Where are we going? Who would want to see me?"

The possibilities raced through my mind like strokes of lightning between earth and cloud.

Who would I wish it to be?

I felt both apprehension and excitement at the possibilities.

"A child," she said, her lips caressing the words.

"A child?"

"A child," she repeated. "Come with me."

The woman turned and walked to a path that led into the trees. I turned to follow and noticed none of the others followed.

"Aren't you coming?"

"No, where you are going you must go alone," a man standing next to the tall man replied.

"Will I see you again?" I asked as the distance between us grew.

"You will see us many more times," the tall man said, waving his hand as he spoke.

The group turned and disappeared into the trees. In our short time together, I felt a bond and was sorry to be separated from them. The words that we would see each other again comforted me.

The woman was walking at a pace that was neither fast nor slow. The rising moon silhouetted her shape and I felt a strong desire to be closer to her. It was not the sexual desire to be with a woman. It was a calling from something deep within me.

The woman stopped and turned to look over her shoulder at me. "Do you remember me?"

"Excuse me," I said.

"Do you remember me?"

"There is something familiar about you. Your eyes remind me of a girl I met, and your smile of a man I know."

The woman's smile grew even broader and her perfect white teeth shone through her lips. "It will come to you."

The woman continued walking and after a few minutes, we entered a small clearing. In the middle of the clearing was a fire with a small child squatting beside it. The child was poking at the coals with a stick.

The woman stopped at the edge of the clearing and motioned toward the child with her hand.

"What is the child's name?" I asked.

The woman smiled and motioned again.

As I stepped out of the trees, the child saw me, and put down the stick.

"Hi. My name is Ty, but my friends call me Blades." I said as I walked towards the child. "What is your name?"

"I don't have name," the child replied as it stood.

I squatted next to the fire and picked up the designated poking stick. The child walked over to me and peered into my eyes. Its face was fair and smooth, and I could not tell if it was a boy or a girl.

"They told me you would tell me the rules," the child said, never breaking its gaze from my face.

The stare of the child was unnerving, and the expectation to know the rules of anything even more uncomfortable. I leaned over and started poking the fire with the stick.

"What rules?"

"The rules of life." the child replied.

"Wow, the rules of life. That is a big one."

I felt uncomfortable, as if Shaman were grilling me once again.

"Who are they?" I asked. "Your parents?"

"Yes, and the others."

"Where are your father and mother?"

"You have met both."

"Was your mother the one that brought me here?" I asked, already knowing the answer. "She is very beautiful."

"Yes. My father is even more beautiful."

I looked into the child's face and realized how beautiful it was.

"Your father must also be beautiful. I can see his beauty, as well as the beauty of your mother, in your face."

The child moved closer, put its hands on the sides of my face, and looked deep into my eyes.

"I can see the face of your father and mother

too."

The honesty of the statement caused my eyes to fill with tears, and I wrapped my arms around the child and pulled it close. The child's arms wrapped around my neck and squeezed as tight as its arms could manage.

"Thank you," I said, fighting back even more tears.

With one gesture, the hands of a child on my face, all barriers were swept away. I leaned back, sat on the ground cross-legged, and put the child on my knee.

"What rules did they tell you I would give you?" I asked, followed by a smile and a wink.

The child's face developed into a broad grin. "The rules of life. I am very young and you are very old. My mother told me you would teach me the most important rules of life."

"She did, did she? The most important rules of life. I have to think about that."

The child watched as I pondered.

There are so many rules of life, what are the most important ones? There are the rules of etiquette and social responsibility, but those would not be the most important rules. There are the rules of how to stay alive, but I think there are rules that are even more important. But what would they be?

I thought about the lessons of Shaman and the girl. I thought about the lessons of parents and friends. I also thought about the lessons I taught myself. As I pondered, the child waited.

"Your question is very difficult and very important. It is a great honor that you would ask me what are the most important rules, and a great responsibility for me to tell you the truth. I do not think I know all the rules of life, so I will tell you the most important rules from what I have learned."

I shifted and put the child on my other knee. "I think there are two rules to life."

"What are the two rules?" the child asked.

"The first rule is that you must be what life created you to be. Life will send you many lessons to teach you how to become what you must be. You must learn each lesson before you can move on to the next lesson. If you have trouble learning a lesson, life will send it to you again in a different form so that you may see it from a different viewpoint to help you learn. Life will keep sending you the lesson in a stronger form until you learn it. It is hard to be who you are, instead of who someone else wants you to be. I spent too much of my life trying to be what I thought other people wanted me to be. What I found out is that I did not know what they wanted. I also learned that for most part, they didn't think of me at all. So, the first rule is, be who you are, not what others want you to be."

"That is a very big rule," the child said.

I rubbed my hand across the child's back. "Yes it is, but it is a simple rule. You will be happy when you are what you were created to be. And unhappy when you try to be something else."

"I will try to be happy," the child said as it smiled and nodded its head. "What is the second rule?"

"The second rule is the secret to life is love. Life is like a game, and the person who loves the most wins. It took me my entire life to learn this rule. Only in the past few days have I come to understand how important love is. I wish I had learned this lesson earlier in life so I could have loved many more than I did. Because I did not love when I had the chance, I lost. We all lost. It is wonderful to love and to be loved. It is the one thing that everyone wants. And remember to love yourself. I was ashamed of some of my thoughts and feelings, and wound up living life like two different people. If I would have loved myself, my life would have been much richer and more enjoyable."

The child rested its head against my chest, yawned and snuggled closer. "Those are very big rules. I will try to remember them."

"I hope you do. I hope you have a wonderful life. I wish I could go with you."

Within a few minutes, the child was asleep, and I was left with my thoughts. Talking to the child reminded me of all the possibilities I felt for life when I was a child. I felt sweet sadness as I realized the child was on the beginning of a great adventure, and I was finishing mine. I regretted not doing more of a great many things, including loving. Love is measured in minutia. A blanket was lying on the log and I pulled it around us. I felt tired, and lay down next to the fire, the child in my arms. I savored the moment, but within minutes, I was asleep, with the child protected in my arms. We slept the sleep of innocents.

CHAPTER 45

Day 4

The sun rising over the ridge awoke me. The child was gone, but the tall man was sitting on the end of the log.

"Good morning," I said as I stretched my arms.

"Good morning. Did you sleep well?"

"Yes very well. Where is the child?"

"The child has gone."

"Did its mother go with it?"

"She goes with all of them."

"All of them?"

"All of them. She is the mother of all children, or did you not recognize her. Has it been that long?"

A flash of recognition washed over me as I remembered her touch, the smell of her breath on my face, the caress of her kiss on my cheek. The memories immersed me in bliss. My eyes closed and a broad smile crossed my face. Her love was all encompassing. Her touch gave me complete reassurance of my value. That was what I felt when she, as a young girl, touched my hand, and again last night when she touched my elbow. It had been so long, that I didn't recognize her touch, until now. Had I become so hardened by life that I could no longer recognize love, let alone initiate it? The thought was replaced by the memory of her touch.

"Will the child be OK?" I asked.

The tall man didn't answer. He looked far into the distance, as if seeking someone to appear out of the mist.

"What is the child's name?" I said.

"It will be called Justin."

"Justin! That's the name of my grandaughter's new baby. I hope his family loves him as much as we love our Justin."

"I am sure they will. He has big shoes to fill. He will grow up strong and develop a strong bond with his parents and grandparents. He will carry that bond to his own family."

The man stopped looking into the distance and turned to look at me. "It is so good to have you back again, Centurion."

A woman in a long, white dress appeared from the trees and offered me a small wooden bowl with broth in it.

"This will give you strength."

I tipped the bowl, and warm broth trickled down my throat, both soothing and comforting. I felt love radiate from the woman, like rays of the sun on my face. Her love was genuine and complete, like that of the tall man. As I drank the broth, others gathered around me adding their love to that of the tall man and the woman. All complete. All genuine. I could feel their love fill me until it started to flow from me back to them. I was genuine, complete. I smiled, my smile reflected in smiles on their faces.

The moment was interrupted when a small man with slight build stepped forward.

"We have a surprise for you."

The man gestured with his left hand toward a path into the trees. The tall man smiled and motioned with his head toward the path. I gave the bowl back to the woman and rose to my feet, not sure I was ready for any more surprises. The morning was young, and already this day had altered the course of everything I knew.

The group followed me as the small man led the way. The path wound through the pine trees, and several times I had to duck under branches that the man in the lead walked under without bending. The small man looked back and chuckled. I didn't know if he was laughing at me having to bend over, or was excited about the surprise. Either way, his laughter was contagious and soon we were both laughing.

The path opened into a clearing, and as we entered the clearing, the small man turned and looked back at me, his eyes beaming.

In the clearing was the most beautiful biplane I had ever seen. The airplane was bright red, and sunlight glistened off its dew-covered wings. On the tail was painted the word Centurion. In the morning sunlight, the airplane embodied the dream of every pilot.

"You have got to be kidding me."

"Do you like it?" the man asked.

"Like it? It's perfect!"

I walked up and ran my hand across the leading edge of the wing, which was smooth as glass. The fabric had been drawn as taught as metal, and the wires between the wings gleamed like polished silver.

I walked around the wing and ran my hand down the fuselage, which was strong and straight. The opening of the cockpit was lined with leather, and inside was a leather-covered seat that looked as comfortable as an overstuffed armchair. The instrument panel had an ignition switch and a tachometer. The controls were stick and rudder.

My hands were shaking as I turned around. "Can I fly it?"

The crowd broke into laughter and I laughed with them.

"I sure hope so," the man replied as he wiped his eyes.

I grabbed the trailing edge of the upper wing with my left hand, put my left foot on the cockpit step, and pulled myself up until I was looking over the top of the wing. I looked past the fuel gauge and propeller, down the length of the meadow and into a clear, blue, sky. Excitement coursed through my veins as the possibility of flight slipped closer. I looked at the sky for what was a fleeting moment to me, but must have seemed hours to those watching. I wanted to stay in that spot between anticipation and realization forever.

I became aware of the gaze of those looking on, and turned to smile the smile of dreams. Some had tears in their eyes, but all were smiling. Everyone knew that I was not only where I longed to be, but also where I was destined to be.

I stepped into the cockpit and lowered my body down into the thick padding of the seat, putting my arms through the shoulder straps, and then slipped the right harness pin into the left harness buckle. The buckle center popped up as the pin snapped into place. I pulled on the shoulder straps, cinching my torso to the seatback.

The man stepped up on the cockpit step and handed me a leather helmet.

I pulled the helmet over my head. "This is great! How did you know?"

The man smiled as he handed me a pair of goggles. "We knew. We have always known. You are the Centurion, and this is your airplane."

"It is perfect!"

"It always is," he said, and then stepped down and walked around to the propeller.

I slipped on the helmet. The helmet was lined with sheepskin and reminded me of the nights I laid on a sheepskin rug in my grandfather's home. My uncle brought the skin from New Zealand, and I wondered if children in New Zealand slept on sheepskins. I would brush my face against the soft surface, and sink my fingers into the long, white hair.

I lifted up the earflaps of the helmet, put on the goggles, and gave the man standing at the propeller a thumbs up sign.

I looked over to the crowd and raised my right thumb, a large smile covering what was left of my face. I pushed the throttle in three times to prime the engine and turned on the ignition switch.

"Contact!"

The man pulled down on the propeller and the engine coughed white smoke, and then fired. I pulled the throttle back to the rear stop, and the engine loped at idle like a racecar tuned to perfection.

The man walked to the end of the left wing and saluted. I returned the salute, and then pushed the throttle forward until the lope smoothed into a roar. The airplane started to roll forward, and I taxied forward enough that I could turn the airplane around without blasting those watching me with prop wash, grass and dirt. I pushed the right rudder pedal and the airplane turned around one hundred eighty degrees. As I taxied to the end of the meadow, I moved the rudder pedals and stick to insure the control surfaces were correct and free. The controls were smooth and light, and when I reached the end of the meadow, I pushed the right rudder pedal hard and the airplane turned around quickly until it was aligned with the meadow. I pulled the throttle back and lowered the earflaps, tying the straps under my chin. The earflaps cut the noise from the exhausts to a low hum.

The group was far enough away that individual members were hard to distinguish. I pushed the throttle forward a little and the airplane started to roll. After a few seconds, I pushed the throttle open halfway. The airplane picked up speed and I pushed the throttle to full open. The acceleration pushed me back in the seat, and my heart began to race. There was no airspeed indicator, but the airplane let me know it was ready to fly. I pulled back on the stick and the plane leapt off the ground into unencumbered flight.

The ground fell away as I climbed toward the blue, and at five hundred feet, I eased the stick forward and pulled the power back. I made a forty-five degree bank turn to the right until I was headed back to the meadow. As I approached I looked for the group, but no one was there. I flew over the meadow and then the trees, searching for anyone, but they had disappeared.

The joy of flight turned into the sorrow of separation. I owed those people so much, yet had failed to say goodbye. Too many times in my life I had overlooked what I had until it was gone, and then lamented not appreciating what I had.

My sorrow was erased by the wind blowing in my face.

Flight! Wonderful, glorious, flight! Freedom!

I pushed the throttle forward, pulled back on the stick, and climbed until the outside air temperature started to drop. The air temperature was comfortable at fifteen hundred feet above the ground. Some pilots fly airplanes. Some pilots wear airplanes. I was one of the latter.

"OK, sweetheart, let's see what we can do."

I pulled back and left on the stick, and pushed the left rudder pedal. The airplane rolled on its side. I pull back on the stick, and the horizon started to move so fast it was hard to follow. The "G" forces pulled my cheeks lower on my face, until I eased the stick forward, then rolled the airplane on its other side. Once again, the horizon crossed my vision so fast it was hard to follow. I let go of the controls and the airplane returned to straight and level flight.

"Yeeeeeehaaaaw!"

I pulled back on the stick until the nose was ten degrees above the horizon and then shoved the stick left and stomped on the left rudder pedal. The airplane rolled all the way around. I did the same thing to the right, and then pushed the throttle and stick forward, picking up speed. When the wires were singing, I pulled the stick all the way back and the airplane pushed up and over, completing the loop with ease. I could not stop smiling.

The sun reflected off the French Broad River like diamonds on blue velvet. The clear blue water that sustained my life beckoned, and my skin tingled as it remembered the cool embrace that made many summer days tolerable.

I pushed the stick forward until I skimmed a few feet above the water. I turned and banked, following the course of the river as it traveled home to the sea. Where land had attempted to hold back the water, the all-powerful river had dissolved rock and moved mountains. I passed a stone cliff, erosion engraved across its face, and further on a white sandy beach, the remnants of what was once a mountain.

I flew down the French Broad River until I passed the waterfall, then circled over the airplane wreckage, which had almost disappeared in grass and vines.

"Goodbye, old friend."

I crossed the Tennessee River, and then hours later the Mississippi as I continued on my journey west. I did not know where I was going, but knew I was headed in the right direction. I watched the fuel gauge, but it never dropped. I reached up and pushed down on it several times to make sure it was working.

I came to the base of the Rockies just before sunset, and landed in a clearing by a stream. When I turned off the ignition switch, silence filled the air. It was so calm it was almost deafening. During the flight, I had explored the cockpit and felt an opening behind the seat. I pulled the seatback forward and found a small space with a blanket and jacket. I was relieved, since I knew travel over the Rockies was going to be cold. Snows had not set in yet, but it was not many days away, and I would have to fly at a higher altitude where the air was colder.

I was not hungry, but the water in the stream was cool and refreshing. I went to sleep under the wing wearing the jacket, covered with the blanket. My sleep was sound and I dreamed of the air blowing across my face. I dreamed of my mother and father, my wife, my son and daughter, and my grandsons and granddaughter. I dreamed the dreams of the blessed.

CHAPTER 46

Day 3

A combination of morning sun and bird songs awoke me. The sleep had refreshed me and I was eager to continue my journey. I took a drink from the stream but still was not hungry. It seemed strange to me that so much of my life had been focused on food, and now it did not seem important.

I put rocks in front and behind the left wheel, then switched on the ignition. When I pulled down on the prop, it took one blade passing before the engine coughed white smoke and fired. In minutes, I was climbing toward the mountains, the air growing colder as I climbed higher and higher. I wound my way through canyons and over passes. Snow covered peaks loomed above me, but never threatened.

I crossed through the Albuquerque valley and out over the high plateau. The plateau dropped off in a spectacular wall that stretched in both directions as far as I could see.

I arrived at the shores of the Pacific Ocean as the sun set. The fuel gauge still showed full and when I landed, I looked inside the tanks. They were both still full to the top. A dramatic sunset filled the sky with all the colors of the rainbow, and the surf lulled me into a deep sleep. In my dreams, I remembered how I had crossed the country, and not seen any signs of human life.

CHAPTER 47

Day 2

Morning brought bright skies and a cool breeze off the ocean. The green flash raced across the sky as the sun rose.

Within minutes of waking, the airplane skipped down the sand, and I turned left, out over the ocean. I still had no idea where I was going, but knew it lay somewhere ahead.

I flew all day, and as night approached, I wondered if I was going to find somewhere to land. The fuel gauge still showed a full tank, but I was concerned that flight at night without instruments was risky business. The sunset displayed another spectacle of grandeur as night fell and the airplane continued on its way west. It seemed to fly itself and I dozed several times, lulled to sleep by the drone of the engine. Each time a small turbulence, or low cloud, awoke me.

The moon was full and the vision of the ocean at night spectacular. Sometime after midnight, the fuel gauge started to bounce in its cap. As I traveled on, the fuel gauge stated to drop, and I knew I was nearing my destination. The gauge was almost on empty when the sun came up behind me, casting long rays that skipped off the waves. When the fuel gauge bottomed out and no longer moved, I knew I was close. I looked out over the propeller and saw an island on the horizon.

On the island was a clearing, and as I lined up for landing, the fuel ran out and the engine became silent. The sound of the wind through the wires comforted me.

I landed and bumped to a stop at the far end of the clearing. I sat in the cockpit and listened to the silence. A wave of gratitude and sorrow swept over me as I thought of how the little airplane had given its all for my journey. It had no more to give, but I also realized that just as I was where I was destined to be, it was where it was destined to be.

I put the jacket behind the seat with the blanket, and then walked toward the middle of the clearing where I had seen a trail as I landed. I did not look back.

The trail, which led up the side of the mountain, wound back and forth as it made its way up. The walk was strenuous but not tiring, and as I approached the top, I turned and looked out over the ocean. The deep blue of the ocean melted into the light blue of sky. I stayed and enjoyed the sight before continuing.

When I reached the top of the mountain, I saw a castle below in a valley. The trail led down to the castle, and before long I stood at the open castle gates. Inside the castle walls, I saw large wooden doors to the right. I entered the doors and found myself in the sanctuary of a church, its wooden pews lined up in two rows. At the end of the sanctuary was an altar with linen altar cloths. It was warm and comfortable, and I sat in one of the pews, absorbing the atmosphere.

After a few minutes, I heard noises to the left of the sanctuary, and when I opened a small door, the noises became louder. As I walked down a stone corridor, the noise increased until I stepped into a great hall. As I stepped into the hall, a loud cheer went up and everyone in the hall rushed to greet me. Everyone I had ever known or met was in the hall. Family, friends, acquaintances, past enemies, all were present, and all were now kin. Hugs and kisses flowed as we greeted each other. A large feast of fruit, vegetables, breads and cheese were set out on a long table. We talked of days gone by, opportunities to say 'I love you' missed, and of love found. The party lasted all day and into the night, with no one seeming to tire. When the moon was high, I felt a familiar presence and stopped to look around the hall.

How could I not feel a familiar presence with all my family and friends around me?

The presence I felt went beyond family and friends, and I sought out each face to see if I could place it. Then I spotted her. Standing in a passage at the far end of the hall, her luminescent green eyes a beacon in the darkness. I walked across the hall toward her, and she smiled at me, the warmth of her love filling the entire hall. As I walked, a silence fell on the hall, like a curtain on a play. When I approached, she stepped into the hall and put out her hand. I slipped my hand into hers and a great cheer arose from behind me.

We turned and walked through the passageway, into the courtyard, past the chapel and out the main gate. I thought of my family and friends still celebrating in the hall behind me, and smiled.

All that was behind me, and I focused on what was ahead. Her hand caressed mine as she looked into my eyes, and I again found the love I had always sought. I realized the search for this love had motivated my entire life. It was the love my parents and grandparents had given me. It was the love I gave my children and grandchildren.

"Are you my mother?" I asked.

The woman stopped and smiled as she leaned over and gave me a kiss on the cheek.

"It is so good to have you home."

She put her arms around me and hugged me. "Nothing compares with holding you in my arms again."

We walked side by side along a path, my hand in hers. The life behind me faded until I remembered nothing. After several hours of walking, we emerged into a clearing with a small fire in the center.

"I have someone I want you to meet," she said.

"Who is it?"

"He is someone you can trust. You are at the beginning of life and he is at the end."

"Why do I need to meet him?"

"He will tell you the rules of life, and you will remind him where he has been."

She stroked my hair, then leaned over and gave me a kiss on the forehead. "I will be back to get you after the two of you have talked. Then we will go on a trip where you will see many new things and meet many new people. I know you will find it fun."

I sat next to the fire and started stirring the coals with a stick. After a while, the woman returned with a tall man that had a kind face.

"Hi, my name is Ty, but my friends call me Blades. What is your name?"

CHAPTER 48

Day 23,512

Wherever you are, I hope you are warm, and dry, and loved.